Chicken Mission

Chaos in Cluckbridge

Jennifer Gray lives in London and Scotland with her husband, four children and a friendly but enigmatic cat. Her other work includes the Atticus Claw series and the Guinea Pigs Online books, co-written with Amanda Swift. The first book in the Atticus series, *Atticus Claw Breaks the Law*, was shortlisted for the Waterstone's Children's Book Prize and won the 2014 Red House Children's Book Award – Younger Readers category.

BY THE SAME AUTHOR

Atticus Claw Breaks the Law
Atticus Claw Settles a Score
Atticus Claw Lends a Paw
Atticus Claw Goes Ashore
Atticus Claw Learns to Draw
Atiticus Claw on the Misty Moor
Atticus Claw Hears a Roar
Chicken Mission: Danger in the Deep Dark Wood
Chicken Mission: Curse of Fogsham Farm
Chicken Mission: Chaos in Cluckbridge

Chicken Mission

Chaos in Cluckbridge

JENNIFER GRAY

ff

FABER & FABER

First published in 2015
by Faber & Faber Limited
Bloomsbury House, 74–77 Great Russell Street,
London WC1B 3DA

Typeset by Crow Books
Printed in the UK by CPI Group (UK) Ltd, Croydon, CR0 4YY

To Peter, David, Paul and John
With special thanks to all at Faber

Prologue

In the bustling metropolis of Cluckbridge, the City Zoo was closing for the night. The head zookeeper was finishing his final round of security checks. Night-time was when the animals were at their most active and it was important to make sure they were all safely locked inside their enclosures before he went home for his supper.

The reptile house was the last place on the zookeeper's list. It gave him the creeps. The head zookeeper could cope with lions and tigers. Logic told him that tarantulas should be wary of *him* and not the other way round. But the reptiles – especially Cleopatra, the queen cobra – scared the pants off him.

Cleopatra was the most formidable animal the head zookeeper had ever come across in all his years at the zoo. The snake was perfectly camouflaged. She could hypnotise her prey with one look of her yellow

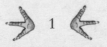

eyes. She was five metres long and could rise up in the air by a third of her length to strike. One bite from her fangs contained enough venom to kill an elephant.

Cleopatra was deadly.

And now it had been confirmed that Cleopatra was about to lay eggs.

The plan was to remove the eggs from Cleopatra as soon as she laid them, and to incubate them in a container until they hatched. Then they would be parcelled out to other zoos around the world to help preserve the species. The head zookeeper was glad *he* didn't have to do it. Of course Cleopatra would be sedated, but when she woke up and saw that her eggs had been taken, she would be furious.

All of a sudden a great clamour went up amongst the animals. The chimps chattered, the night birds hooted and from the direction of the lion house came a threatening growl. The head zookeeper felt the hairs on his neck prickle. Hastily he gave the door of the reptile house a quick tug to make sure it was securely locked, then let himself out of the

front gates of the zoo and snapped the padlock shut
behind him.

Inside the reptile house, the animals heard the
metallic scrape of the bolts being drawn across the
gates and the chink of the padlock.

'He'ssssss gone, Cleopatra,' whispered the python.

'Ssssssso will I be ssssssssoon,' came a soft hiss in
reply.

'Remember to leave your sssssskin behind ssssssso
your keeper doesn't notice you're missssssssing when
he comesssssss to feed you in the morning,' the
python advised.

'Very well,' came the whispered response. 'I will
do it now.'

The queen cobra flexed her coils, then she went
completely limp. Very slowly, head first, she began
to slip out of her old skin, emerging from it inch by
perfect inch. Her new skin was identical to the old,
with exactly the same brown and yellow markings.

She was still perfectly camouflaged against the bed of leaves and twigs.

With a final slither, the last loop of her tail came free. Cleopatra turned her head and regarded the shed skin. It would fool her keeper for a while.

Cleopatra let out a long hiss. She had to lay her eggs in private: somewhere the humans couldn't take them from her.

She moved quickly to the back of the enclosure, where the snakes were fed through a hatch.

There! She flicked her tongue out and inserted the forks into the lock. *Click!* With a quick twist the lock opened. The hatch swung back with a creak. She poked her head through it into a narrow corridor with a concrete floor.

Heating pipes ran along the length of the corridor, letting out a faint gurgling and hammering as the water chugged through them. Cleopatra's tongue flicked in and out. On it she caught the scent of fresh air. She raised her head. A draught was coming from above the pipes where a window had been left ajar.

Freedom, thought Cleopatra, *at lasssssst*.

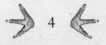

'Goodbye, Cleopatra. Good luck,' hissed the python.

Cleopatra barely heard him. She slipped through the hatch, climbed up the water pipes and disappeared through the open window into the dark night.

Chapter One

'Done!' Amy Cluckbucket stuffed the final bits and pieces into her suitcase and banged the lid shut. 'Phew!' she lay back on her straw bed with her legs in the air. Amy wasn't a very tidy chicken, and packing was hard work: even harder than being a chicken agent, in fact. There were so many things to remember, like her toothbrush and her bandana. Not to mention all the things she wanted to show her parents, like her Certificate of Egg-cellence from the Kung Fu School of Poultry and two editions of the *Daily Snail* which had pictures of her on the front page.

Amy was part of an elite chicken squad whose job it was to defeat chicken predators. Together with her two friends, Boo and Ruth, she had been trained to become a chicken warrior at the Kung Fu School of Poultry in Tibet before arriving at Chicken HQ to meet their mentor, Professor Rooster. Since then Amy, Boo and Ruth had completed two successful

missions against Thaddeus E. Fox and his MOST WANTED Club of villains. And Professor Rooster was so pleased with their good work that he had decided to give them a holiday.

That meant Amy was going home to Perrin's Farm for the first time in months. She couldn't wait to see her parents and tell them about her adventures.

'All ready, Amy?' Ruth sat down beside her. Ruth was a tall, white chicken with spectacles and a grey scarf.

'Yep,' said Amy. She sat up. 'Where's your suitcase, Ruth? Haven't you packed yet?'

'I don't need to,' Ruth said. She waved a remote control at Amy. 'Behold! The world's first self-packing suitcase!'

Amy looked around Chicken HQ. Ruth's suitcase lay on the floor between the laptop and the gadgets cupboard. A large magnet on a metal arm emerged from inside the case. Ruth pressed a button on the remote control. Various objects flew towards the magnet and landed in the suitcase, including Ruth's spectacles.

'Barn it, now I can't see!' said Ruth.

Amy went to retrieve the spectacles. Ruth was brilliant at inventing things, but sometimes she didn't get it quite right first time. 'What about you, Boo?' Amy asked. 'Are you nearly ready?'

'Nearly,' Boo said. 'I'm just brushing my boots!' Boo had beautiful honey-coloured feathers which, unlike most chickens', went all the way down to her toes. Boo's lovely thick coat always made Amy feel slightly self-conscious about her own appearance – Amy was a small brown chicken with lots of fluffy grey feathers around her tummy and scrawny pink legs – but she knew that chickens come in all shapes and sizes so she didn't really mind.

Amy bent down to collect the spectacles then squinted at the sun through one of the shed windows. Chicken HQ consisted of three dilapidated potting sheds located in an old walled garden on the Dudley Estate. The sheds were joined together inside to make an operations room. Of course, the humans who lived at Dudley Manor had no idea what was in there. It was the chickens' secret!

The sun was low in the sky, which meant it was nearly time for their flight. 'The albatross will be here any minute,' Amy said excitedly, straightening up. She gave Ruth back her spectacles. 'Are you sure you don't want to come with me to Perrin's Farm?' she asked her friend.

'Not this time, Amy,' Ruth said. 'Boo already asked me to go and stay at her Aunt Mildred's in Cluckbridge, and I always wanted to see the city.'

Ruth couldn't go home to her parents because they lived too far away, which was why she had accepted an invitation from Boo's aunt to stay with her instead for the holiday. 'I'll come next time, I promise,' she added.

'So will I,' Boo said, coming over, 'if I'm invited.' She gave Amy a wink.

'Of course you are!' Amy had once felt a bit shy around Boo and Ruth – they were so sophisticated compared to her – but now she didn't. Each of the chickens had a special skill: Boo's was perseverance, Ruth's was intelligence, and Amy's was courage. Together the three of them made a great team.

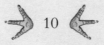

A shadow passed across the windows.

'There's the albatross!' cried Amy.

She grabbed her suitcase, threw on her backpack and rushed out of the nearest potting-shed door. Cluckbridge wasn't very far from Perrin's Farm. The albatross was going to drop her off first and then take Boo and Ruth on to the city. In just an hour or so she would be home!

She was about to climb on board the albatross when Ruth called her back. 'Amy, come here a minute,' she said.

'What is it?' Amy asked. Ruth's face wore a worried expression.

'It's Professor Rooster. He's on the laptop. I think he's got another mission for us.'

Chapter Two

Reluctantly, Amy stepped away from the albatross and trudged back to the potting sheds. She hoped this wouldn't mean she couldn't go on holiday.

The laptop stood in the middle of Chicken HQ on an old wooden crate. Boo and Ruth sat beside it on garden stools. Amy dragged herself over to the third stool and plonked her bottom on it. Maybe the professor just wanted to wish them happy holidays, she thought hopefully.

Professor Rooster was staring out at them from the laptop screen. As soon as she saw the stern look on his face, Amy knew it was something important. Her head drooped in disappointment. She *was* going to miss her holiday after all. Then she remembered the monitor was two-way and that the Professor could see her, so she lifted her chin up and tried to look brave.

'Chickens,' he said, 'thank goodness I caught you. Something terrible has happened.'

'What is it this time, Professor?' asked Ruth.

The professor drew himself up. 'It is my duty to inform you that Cleopatra, the queen cobra, has escaped from Cluckbridge City Zoo,' he said.

Boo gasped. 'Cleopatra!'

'Yes, Boo, I'm afraid so,' the professor said. His voice was gentle.

'Oh, no!' Boo started to cry.

Amy looked from Professor Rooster to Boo and back again in puzzlement. 'What's the matter with Boo?' she whispered to Ruth. 'Did I miss something?'

Ruth shrugged. 'I don't know,' she replied.

'Boo already knows about Cleopatra from personal experience,' Professor Rooster said. 'I will leave it to her to tell you about it if she chooses. But for the benefit of you, Ruth, and you, Amy,' he pointed at them in turn, 'let me fill you in.'

They waited. Something told Amy this was one of the most serious things that had ever happened in her young chicken life. She listened carefully.

'A queen cobra is probably the most deadly animal in the world,' said the professor. 'It can hypnotise its

prey with a look and kill with one injection of venom. Cleopatra isn't just any queen cobra, however, she has a track record. She is known to have attacked her human keeper at the zoo on a number of occasions. She is also reported by my spies in Cluckbridge to have consumed over twenty full-grown chickens in the past year. And I should tell you, chickens, that she doesn't always bother to kill them first.'

Amy felt faintly sick. She put her wing round Boo, who was still sobbing quietly. Amy gave her a squeeze.

'This is what Cleopatra looks like,' the professor said.

Amy started as a picture of a terrifying snake showed up on the screen. Cleopatra was dark brown with a yellowish throat and a great hood. She stared right out at Amy from the laptop. Even thought it was only a photograph, Amy felt she was being drawn in by the snake's cold, mesmerising stare.

'We're not entirely sure how she escaped,' the professor said. 'The human newspapers are reporting that Cleopatra's keeper may have forgotten to lock the

cage properly. That seems unlikely to me. I suspect that Cleopatra's been planning this for a while.' He gave a little cough. 'You see, chickens, unfortunately it's not just Cleopatra we have to worry about . . .'

'You don't mean Thaddeus E. Fox and the MOST WANTED Club have teamed up with her as well, do you?' Amy squawked.

'No, no,' the professor said hastily. 'Thaddeus and

his gang haven't been seen since your last successful mission.'

Amy let out a sigh of relief. Thank goodness for that!

'The problem is, Cleopatra is expecting babies,' said the professor. 'Any day now, she's going to lay eggs.'

'Eggs?' Amy exclaimed. She'd never really thought about how snakes had babies before, but the fact they laid eggs came as a complete surprise. 'What, like a hen?'

'Yes, Amy, like a hen, except whereas a hen will only lay one egg at a time, Cleopatra will lay a large number all at once.'

'How many is a large number, Professor?' asked Ruth.

'Anywhere between 30 and 50,' said Professor Rooster.

There was a stunned silence. Boo had stopped crying. She wiped her beak on a tissue.

Amy gave her a reassuring pat.

'Cleopatra doesn't want to lose her babies. She will

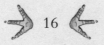

do anything to stop the humans at the zoo getting hold of her eggs in case they donate them to other zoos around the world,' Professor Rooster said. 'But she doesn't have much time. My gut feeling is she's still in Cluckbridge. Her instinct will be to lie low somewhere dark and quiet in the city where there's plenty of food. That way she can build a nest and incubate the eggs until they hatch . . .'

Amy opened her beak to say something but Professor Rooster held up his wing.

'Before you ask, Amy, yes, a snake does sit on her eggs like a hen.'

'Oh,' said Amy. 'Thank you.'

'In the meantime, no chicken in the area will be safe; nor will any chick. Cleopatra is used to being fed them live by the keeper, but she's more than capable of catching them herself.' He looked directly at Boo. 'That includes the rest of your family, Boo.'

The rest of Boo's family? What did he mean? Amy wondered.

Boo nodded. 'I understand,' she said quietly.

'Very well,' the rofessor said. 'Your mission,

chickens, is to fly to Cluckbridge, find Cleopatra and return her to the City Zoo. If she has already laid her eggs, then you must return them too. It is vital, I repeat, *vital* that you stop those eggs from hatching outside the zoo. Otherwise, no chicken in the area will be safe.'

'What about our holiday?' Amy burst out. As soon as she'd said it, she wished she hadn't.

'The mission comes first, Amy,' Professor Rooster reminded her sharply. 'Chickens' lives are at stake. No one is taking a holiday until this is over. Do you understand?'

'Yes, Professor,' Amy replied. She hadn't meant to sound sulky and silly but she was so disappointed she wouldn't be able to see her parents that she couldn't help it.

'I hope so,' said Professor Rooster. 'All three of you will be staying with Boo's Aunt Mildred until further notice. Amy, I've already informed your parents that you won't be able to join them at Perrin's Farm this time.'

Amy felt a tear trickle down her cheek. She hadn't

realised how much she missed Perrin's Farm until she suddenly wasn't allowed to go. She felt a wing steal round her shoulders.

'Hey!' It was Ruth. 'Cheer up. You'll be able to go and see them when the mission's over.'

Amy nodded glumly. Only if they defeated Cleopatra, she thought. If they failed, she might never see her parents again.

'Remember, whatever you do, don't make eye contact with Cleopatra or she'll hypnotise you,' Professor Rooster told them. 'And watch out for her tongue. That's how she senses things if she can't see them. Not by taste, but by smell.'

'How will we keep in touch?' asked Ruth.

'Aunt Mildred has access to a computer if you need to contact me,' Professor Rooster replied. 'In the meantime, I'll tell my spies to keep an eye out for any sign of Cleopatra. Any news, I'll let you know by pigeon post.'

'What gadgets should we take?' asked Ruth.

'I've put some things to help you in the Emergency Chicken Pack,' Professor Rooster said. 'The mite

blaster won't work on Cleopatra's scales, so you'll need to use other weapons against her. Good luck, chickens.' Professor Rooster leaned forward towards his computer screen and turned it off. The screen fizzled with grey and white lines and then went black.

Chapter Three

Down in a burrow in the Deep Dark Woods on the edge of the Dudley Estate, Thaddeus E. Fox was fast asleep in his feather bed, when there was a knock on the door.

'Go away,' Thaddeus growled.

There was a pause, then the knock came again.

'I'm not here,' Thaddeus said.

'Yes, you are,' a posh voice replied.

Thaddeus groaned. The posh voice sounded very much as if it belonged to his old school pal, Snooty Bush. Thaddeus wasn't very keen on Snooty Bush at the best of times but right now, what with everything that had happened lately, Snooty Bush was positively the last fox in the world he wanted to see. He couldn't bear the humiliation. He buried his head under the duvet and put his paws over his ears.

BASH! BASH! BASH!

'Let me in!' the voice demanded.

'Or what?' Thaddeus shouted back at it.

'Or I'll huff and I'll puff and I'll blow your house down!' Snooty Bush chortled.

'Ha, ha, ha,' said Thaddeus sarcastically. 'Tell you what, how about I light the fire and you come down the chimney?'

'Ah, come on, old man,' Snooty Bush pleaded. 'Stop mucking about. I've got something to tell you. It's important.'

'Oh, very well!' Thaddeus rose from his bed, pulled a grubby dressing gown around his shoulders and shuffled towards the door. He unbolted it top and bottom and turned the handle. The door creaked open.

Snooty Bush stood on the doorstep of the burrow looking as jaunty as ever. He was wearing the traditional Eat'em College for Gentlemen Foxes' uniform – top hat, a jacket with tails and a smart waistcoat. His face registered shock when he saw Thaddeus's scruffy appearance. 'Blimey!' he exclaimed. 'What happened to you?'

'It's a long story.' Thaddeus said.

'I'd better come in then so you can tell me.'

Before Thaddeus could stop him, Snooty Bush had pushed past him into the burrow. Thaddeus closed the door with a sigh.

'Well?' Snooty Bush said, looking round the burrow in distaste. 'Are you going to tell me what happened?'

Thaddeus followed his eye. The burrow did look a bit of a mess he had to admit. The floor was

covered in crumbs, the larder was empty, dirty dishes soaked in a sink full of filthy washing-up water, and a rancid smell came from the direction of the toilet. He realised with a jolt of shame that Snooty Bush must think he'd turned into a complete slob. 'It's the chickens' fault,' he said sulkily.

'What chickens?'

Thaddeus remembered that the last time he saw Snooty Bush was just before the MOST WANTED Club's first defeat at the wings of Professor Rooster's elite chicken squad at the Eat'em College Annual Dinner. He told Snooty Bush what happened after he had left.

'You got dowsed in custard?' Snooty Bush said incredulously.

Thaddeus nodded. 'And blasted with mites.'

'That must have been itchy!' Snooty Bush shook his head in sympathy.

'It was, especially as the mites seemed to be attracted to the custard,' Thaddeus recalled, with a shudder. 'The second time was even worse, though.'

'The second time?'

Thaddeus told him about that too. 'Have you ever

had cowpat in your whiskers? Or up your nose?' he whispered.

'Can't say I have,' Snooty Bush murmured.

Thaddeus's shoulders started to shake. In spite of his misgivings about Snooty Bush, it felt good to talk to someone: he'd been cooped up in the burrow by himself managing on leftovers for so long now that he couldn't actually remember when it was he'd last seen another animal's face.

'It's all right, old man,' Snooty Bush said soothingly. 'You can trust me. I promise I won't tell anyone.'

'I'm scared to go out in case they attack again!' Thaddeus confessed. 'Me! Thaddeus E. Fox, the MOST WANTED villain in the MOST WANTED Club. Scared of three kid chickens!' He shook his head sorrowfully.

Snooty Bush patted him on the shoulder. 'What happened to the other villains?' he asked.

'They ditched me,' sobbed Thaddeus. Now that he'd started his confession, he couldn't stop. 'Tiny Tony Tiddles – the cat with the hat – he said I was all washed up. He left to join a gang of farm cats.'

25

'That's awful.'

Thaddeus nodded. 'Remember Kebab Claude, the poodle?'

'The one who was good at barbecues?'

'Yes, well he said he didn't want to hang out with me any more. He found a home with a butcher who makes his own sausages.'

'Handy for him, I suppose,' said Snooty Bush tactfully. 'What about the Pigeon Poo Gang?'

'They decided to go it alone! Last I heard they were hanging about the local porridge factory, trying to raid packets of oats.'

'I see.'

'They don't need me any more!' Thaddeus howled. 'They think I'm useless at being a villain.'

'There, there.' Snooty Bush fished inside his waistcoat and handed Thaddeus a red cotton handkerchief.

Thaddeus blew on it loudly. 'Thanks,' he said gruffly.

'Look, old man. You and I haven't always seen eye to eye, but we're both Old Eat'emians and Old Eat'emians stick together,' Snooty Bush said firmly.

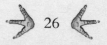

'I suppose . . .' Thaddeus agreed glumly.

'What you need is a change of scene,' Snooty Bush declared. 'Get your confidence back. Then, when you're feeling better, you can start up the MOST WANTED Club again and catch those beastly chickens.' He leaned forward. 'Talking of which, that reminds me what I came to see you about.'

'What was that, then?' Thaddeus was beginning to feel a bit better. It was good to get things off his chest.

'Remember I moved to the city a little while back?' Snooty Bush said.

'Yes.' Thaddeus was listening keenly.

'It's great fun – such a happening place. A real melting pot. And there are loads of chickens.' Snooty Bush snorted. 'The humans keep them in their gardens!'

Thaddeus pricked up his ears. *Now that sounded interesting.* 'Go on,' he said.

'Well this year the Society of Enterprising Foxes is holding its Annual Convention at Cluckbridge.'

'So?'

'The Society encourages foxes to think big,'

Snooty Bush explained, 'especially when it comes to catching chicken. Look at this.' Snooty Bush fumbled in his other pocket and removed a piece of paper, which he placed on the table. He smoothed it out with a paw.

You are warmly invited to

The Society of Enterprising Foxes Annual Convention and Dinner

At Cluckbridge City Railway Depot

Drinks!

Chicken Dinner!

Speeches!

Foxy Singsong!

Surprise Guest!

PS: Please note that in celebration of the Society's tenth anniversary, this year's Convention will include a prize for the most enterprising fox. All devious plans on how to catch the most chickens should be submitted to the Chairfox by Thursday.

'What's the prize?' Thaddeus's yellow eyes had assumed some of their old cunning. When it came to catching chickens, he was ace at devious plans. (Well, he used to be before Professor Rooster's elite chicken squad started spoiling everything.)

'If you win, the Society helps put your plan into practice,' said Snooty Bush. He leaned forward. 'Think about it, Thaddeus, it's a huge opportunity. Instead of catching the odd chicken here and there, there'd be a whole machine behind us with all the fox-power we need to turn our devious plan into a proper business. And I've had an idea.'

'What?' Thaddeus demanded. The thought of catching chickens had got his juices flowing.

'We could run a chicken farm! Right there in the city,' Snooty Bush said excitedly.

'A chicken farm?' Thaddeus echoed.

'Yes! Think about it. We'll be rich! Our loyal customers will steal anything we ask for from the humans: diamonds, feather cushions, toothpaste, Stilton cheese – you name it! All we need to do is to come up with a plan of how to make it work;

the Society will help us put it into action. Come on, Thaddeus,' Snooty Bush urged. 'Say you'll do it! Say you'll be my partner.'

Thaddeus E. Fox was thinking hard. *A chicken farm?!* It was a brilliant idea. *If they could catch enough chickens and find somewhere to hide them out of sight of the humans.* Thaddeus E. Fox grinned. *Of course they could!* His confidence had returned. He was certain he'd come up with a suitably devious plan once he got away from the Deep Dark Woods to the bright lights of Cluckbridge.

'All right!' he agreed. 'You've got yourself a deal!'

Chapter Four

The albatross flew over Cluckbridge.

Amy had never seen anything like it. The city was crowded with buildings. Its streets were full of shops and houses at one end and skyscrapers at the other. Cars whizzed up and down the busy roads. Humans hurried along the pavements. A river meandered through the city's heart. Trains thundered across it on steel bridges, while long boats carrying big containers puttered up and down its length.

The albatross flew lower.

'There's the City Zoo,' Ruth said, pointing it out.

Amy pulled her super-spec headset down over her eyes so that she could zoom in for a better view. The City Zoo was beside a big park, north of the river. Iron railings ran around the edge. Inside the railings the animals were housed in a mixture of old brick buildings and outdoor enclosures decorated with rocks and trees.

Amy spotted a lion standing on a rock. She gasped. She had only ever seen a lion in pictures before. If Cleopatra was scarier than that, she didn't know what they'd do!

The albatross flew on away from the bustling city centre to where tall, thin houses fronted onto the streets. There were no gaps between the houses, but they had long oblong gardens at the back, separated by wooden fences. Amy was excited to see that a few of them contained chicken coops.

The albatross swooped low over one garden fence and landed with a bump in a vegetable patch amongst some runner beans.

'Sorry about that,' the albatross apologised. 'There's not much of a runway to work with. Remember to take all your luggage with you.'

'We will.' Amy hoisted the Emergency Chicken Pack over one wing. 'Thanks for the ride.' The three chickens slid off the albatross clutching their suitcases, their backpacks on their shoulders.

They picked their way through the runner bean canes towards the chicken coop. The coop was at

the bottom of the garden under an apple tree on a patch of bare ground. It was ringed with two loops of chicken wire.

'Boo!' a voice cried. A smart chicken scuttled out from behind the apple tree, where several chickens were admiring the blossom, and trotted towards the gate. She looked very much like Boo, except that she had thick cream feathers instead of thick honey-coloured ones.

'Aunt Mildred!' Boo threw down her luggage and ran towards her aunt.

'How lovely to see you, dear!' Aunt Mildred said. 'And your friends. Hang on a minute while I let you in.'

Aunt Mildred began to untwist a loop of chicken wire with her beak. 'Wait, I'll have to go and get the pliers,' she said.

Amy puffed out her cheeks. It would take them all day to get in at this rate, even with pliers! 'Why don't we use the flight-booster engines?' she suggested.

'Good idea,' Ruth agreed.

The three chickens strapped themselves into the machines and helicoptered over the fence.

Aunt Mildred was amazed. 'How fantastic!' she said. 'We could do with some of those to get about. I don't suppose you've got any spare, have you?'

'I'm afraid not, Aunt Mildred,' Boo replied.

Aunt Mildred sighed. 'It used to be so easy here to visit friends. We'd just squeeze under the garden fence and off we'd go, but these days this place is like a prison.'

Aunt Mildred gave Boo a big hug and shook wings with Ruth and Amy.

'I don't remember the security being this tight before,' Boo observed. 'When did the humans put up chicken wire?'

Aunt Mildred shook her head sorrowfully and said, 'When the foxes appeared in Cluckbridge. Honestly, Boo, the city isn't a safe place to be a chicken any more.'

'Where do the foxes live?' asked Boo.

Aunt Mildred shrugged. 'Who knows? Wherever they live, there are certainly plenty of them. We chickens barely ever get together any more. And we used to have such brilliant street parties in the old days.'

'Why don't the humans get rid of them?' asked Amy. 'The farmer at the farm where I used to live scared them away with a gun.'

'They're not allowed to do that here. The city's not at all like the country.' Aunt Mildred gave a little shudder. 'Foxes are a real problem. So are the rats.'

'Rats!' Amy echoed. She had no idea the city was such a dangerous place to live. 'I didn't know you had rats.'

'They're everywhere,' said Aunt Mildred. 'I reckon you can't go ten metres in Cluckbridge without being close to a rat. They're not as bold as the foxes but they're there, all right. They sneak in and take our eggs when we're not looking. Most of them hang out in the sewers, where it's smelly.'

'Yuk,' said Amy.

'But then you three won't be scared of a few rats and the odd fox or two after your adventures!' Aunt Mildred's face brightened. 'Now come in. I want to hear all about what you've been up to.'

The three chickens followed her up the wooden ramp into the coop.

It was the cleanest, tidiest coop Amy had ever seen in her life. On one wall hung two large roosting boxes – one above the other – full of fresh-scented hay, with a little set of steps for the chickens to climb up and down. Beneath the roosting boxes was a food trough stuffed with mealworm and a clean bowl of water in case the chickens felt thirsty. Tucked away discreetly in the opposite corner was a nesting place in a recess.

'That's where we go to lay eggs,' Aunt Mildred explained, when she saw Amy looking at it. 'You can use it if you like.'

'Thank you,' Amy said politely. She still hadn't laid her first egg, mainly because she'd been too busy having adventures, but she really wanted to. And the nesting place looked the ideal spot to do it.

'How's the collection coming on?' asked Boo.

'Wonderfully well, thank you!' Aunt Mildred said. She saw the look of perplexity on Amy and Ruth's faces. 'The humans treat us as pets,' Aunt Mildred said. 'They give us all sorts of interesting things to play with when they're away at work. At weekends they even let us roam inside the house. They think

 37

it's amusing when we pick up bits and pieces around the place. Usually they let us keep them. They don't realise what we use them for!'

Aunt Mildred opened a cupboard.

Amy gasped. Inside the cupboard were all sorts of wonderful things. She glimpsed shiny tin foil, a nailbrush, a bell, long loops of colourful wool, knitting needles, ribbon, a box of tacks, stamps, pencils, paper, a book of Sudoku, a toolkit, a selection of badges, some Lego bricks, an assortment of Scrabble tiles, an alarm clock and a few tablets of soap.

'Do you have any more books?' asked Ruth hopefully, leafing through the puzzle book.

Amy glanced over Ruth's shoulder. Most of the puzzles had been completed. Amy thought Aunt Mildred and her friends must be very brainy.

'Oh yes,' Aunt Mildred said. She scratched some straw away from the floor of the coop and pulled at a floorboard. 'We keep them in the library in case the humans suspect anything.'

The library?! Amy peered down. Beneath the floorboards books were stacked upright in neat piles

with little walkways between them so that you could see the spines. 'Where do you get the books *from*?' she asked in bewilderment. She didn't think even Professor Rooster would have as many books as that in his secret hideout on the Dudley Estate.

Aunt Mildred shrugged. 'This is just a fraction of what the humans throw away. They leave them outside in a cardboard box for recycling. It's just a matter of choosing which ones we haven't read yet.

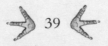

We've got a radio too,' she said proudly. 'It picks up the Bird Broadcasting Corporation. We get most channels, although we mainly listen to the news. That's how we've been following what you three have been up to.'

'Cool!' said Amy. 'Er . . . you don't happen to have an Eggs-Box do you?' Books weren't really her thing; nor was the radio for that matter. She preferred playing computer games, especially Chicken World Wrestling 3.

'Not in the coop,' Aunt Mildred said. 'There's one in the house, though. You could have a go at the weekend when the humans aren't looking.'

The mention of the weekend checked Amy's enthusiasm. She wondered dismally if she would be alive by then. They still had Cleopatra to catch.

'Oh!' Boo exclaimed. 'You've kept all my old gymnastics equipment!'

Amy glanced over. Stuffed into another cupboard were a stack of plastic plant pots, a selection of forked sticks, a roll of foam and several pieces of bamboo pole.

'Please set it up,' Amy begged her. 'I'd love to see you do gymnastics properly.'

'Yes, go on, Boo,' Ruth urged.

'I'll bet you've improved a lot since you were last at home,' Aunt Mildred smiled.

But Boo shook her head. 'Maybe later.' She took hold of Aunt Mildred's wing and steered her towards a little table.

Amy and Ruth followed. The four chickens sat down.

'The thing is, Aunt Mildred, we're not actually here on holiday any more. We're here on a mission.'

'Ah,' said Aunt Mildred, her face serious. 'It's to do with Cleopatra, isn't it?'

'I heard about Cleopatra's escape on the radio,' Aunt Mildred said. 'I was so worried when I heard the news, especially after what happened to your poor dear mother, Boo.'

Amy and Ruth exchanged glances.

Was that why Boo had been so upset when Professor Rooster told them about the mission? Was it something to do with her mother? They waited.

'The others don't know, Aunt Mildred,' Boo said.

'I think you'd better tell them, dear, don't you?' Aunt Mildred said quietly.

Boo nodded. She took a deep breath and turned to Amy and Ruth. 'Look, I'm sorry I didn't tell you before, but my mother, Aunt Mildred and me, well, believe it or not, we're ex-bats.'

'You used to be bats?' Amy asked. 'I don't get it.'

'No, Amy,' Ruth said. 'That's not what Boo means. A "bat" is a short name for a battery hen. An

ex-bat is a hen that used to be one.'

'Oh,' said Amy. Amy knew what a battery hen was. All chickens did. It was the one thing they feared becoming more than anything else. Battery hens were forced to live in cramped cages in dark warehouses, laying egg after egg after egg and never ever going outside once in their whole entire lives. Amy was a free-range chicken, which meant when she was growing up at Perrin's Farm she had mainly lived outside in the farmyard or played in the barn with her friends. But she had often heard her parents remark in low voices how lucky they were compared to battery hens. She could hardly believe that Boo had been one.

'Why didn't you tell us before?' she asked her friend.

'I don't really know. I suppose I thought you might not like me very much if you knew.'

'That's silly!' Amy exclaimed. 'Of course we'd like you just the same!'

'Or even more,' Ruth said. 'I mean, it's pretty amazing that you got through that to become a chicken warrior! I'm not sure I would have.'

'Thanks,' Boo said, blushing.

'But what happened to your mother?' Amy felt she could ask Boo about her now that they'd cleared the air. She still couldn't work out what being an ex-bat had got to do with Cleopatra.

'I . . . It's so hard to talk about it,' Boo said.

'Shall I tell them, dear?' asked Aunt Mildred.

'Yes, please,' Boo said.

'Boo's mum and I were once show hens,' Aunt Mildred began. 'But our breeder lost interest and sold us to a farmer who pretended he'd take care of us. In fact, he ran a battery farm.' She shuddered. 'I can't explain to you how awful that place was. There were four of us to a cage less than one metre square, and hundreds of cages all stacked one on top of the other. The humans would take our eggs the minute we laid them but somehow Boo's mum managed to hide Boo from them. That's how Boo came to grow up inside the barn. But then Boo's mother stopped laying eggs. And when a chicken couldn't lay eggs any more, the farmer got rid of it. He put it in a cage with the others who were too weak to lay. Then a van would come from the City Zoo to pick them up.'

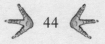

'The zoo?' Amy echoed.

'Yes, Amy,' Boo said in a choked voice. 'They were taken to feed Cleopatra. Apparently she wouldn't eat eggs or dead mice like the other snakes did; she wanted fresh chicken.'

Amy and Ruth listened in horror. Silence descended on the group of chickens while they thought about Boo's mum. 'How did you and Aunt Mildred escape?' Amy asked eventually.

'The farm was closed down. We were taken to an animal welfare centre to be cared for. We were a sight, I can tell you. We'd lost all our feathers from where we'd been crowded together in the tiny cages.'

'No feathers!' Amy exclaimed. She could hardly believe it. Now Boo and Aunt Mildred had the most beautiful feathers she had ever seen! She supposed that was because Aunt Mildred and Boo's mum had once been show chickens.

'It's true,' said Boo. 'I was almost completely bald.'

'We were lucky,' Aunt Mildred said. 'Boo and I were adopted with a few of our friends by some kind humans who lived in the city. They brought us here.

Once we got used to being free to roam again, we wanted to make up for lost time. That's why we started to collect things and read and do crosswords and have street parties – and why Boo took up gymnastics. We wanted to make the most of our freedom. It was so precious to us after what we'd been through.'

Amy could see now why Boo spent so long preening her feathers. She could also see why her friend's special skill was perseverance. Boo and Aunt Mildred and the other ex-bats had never given up, not ever, even when it seemed like they would never get out of the battery farm.

'That's why I was so upset when Professor Rooster told us about Cleopatra,' Boo said.

'Did Professor Rooster know all of this?' Ruth asked.

Boo shrugged. 'Professor Rooster knows everything,' she said.

'We'll find Cleopatra, Boo,' Ruth promised. 'Don't worry. We won't let her hurt any more of your family. Or any other chickens in Cluckbridge.'

'I was just coming to that. That's the wonderful thing,' Aunt Mildred said. 'You don't have to do the mission!'

'What?' Amy exclaimed. 'Why not?'

'Cleopatra has left Cluckbridge! Look! It's in the humans' evening paper. The pigeons dropped off a copy at lunchtime.'

'Where's Mumbai?' Amy asked.

'In India,' Ruth replied.

'That's where Cleopatra's from originally,' Aunt Mildred explained. 'She's gone home to lay her eggs. The boat left at ten o'clock this morning.'

'You mean she's gone for good?' Boo gasped.

Aunt Mildred nodded. 'Yes.'

'Hooray!' The three chickens rejoiced.

Boo's eyes shone with relief.

'You know what that means, don't you?' Amy could hardly contain her excitement.

The others looked at her questioningly.

'We *can* have a holiday after all!'

Chapter Six

Down by the Cluckbridge Railway Depot, it was nearly time for the Society for Enterprising Foxes Annual Convention. Thaddeus E. Fox was practising his acceptance speech. He and Snooty Bush hadn't actually *won* the prize for the most enterprising foxes yet, but Thaddeus was confident that they soon would.

Their devious plan wasn't just enterprising, it was totally fox-tastic.

He checked his watch; it was five to midnight. The Convention started in a few minutes. It was being held in the dining car of one of the humans' trains, which had been parked at the Depot overnight.

The dining car was already full of foxes. For those still filing in through the carriage doors it was standing room only. Music blasted from a stereo system. Snooty Bush was right, Thaddeus thought: the city was a happening place if you were a fox.

He was pleased to note that, if anything, the vixens outnumbered the dogs. Thaddeus believed in fox equality. Everyone would have an equal chance of helping them put their devious plan for killing chickens into action once he and Snooty Bush were announced the winners.

Just then a clock chimed midnight. The music went quiet.

One of the vixens jumped up onto the bar.

'Ladies and gentlemen,' she began, 'welcome to the Society for Enterprising Foxes. It's great to see such a good turnout tonight. Later we will be feasting on some of those pampered pet chickens we've all become so fond of . . .'

A great cheer went up.

'Followed by a singsong to some of our favourite foxy pop tunes . . .'

Another great cheer went up.

'But first, to our tenth anniversary competition! Who will be crowned the Society of Enterprising Foxes' Most Enterprising Fox?'

An expectant hush fell on the room.

'This is it, old man. Paws crossed,' Snooty Bush whispered.

'Thank you to everyone who took part,' the vixen said. 'The committee received a large number of entries from which we have selected the best three. These will go forward to tonight's final.'

A growl of anticipation rose from the excited audience.

'The first of our finalists is Owen Fox Boxer with his devious plan to break into Harrisons supermarket stores and steal all the frozen chickens from the refrigerators.'

There was a big round of applause for Owen Fox Boxer.

'Pathetic,' Thaddeus sneered under his breath. 'What happens when they all defrost at the same time? You can't eat them all at once.'

'The second of our finalists is Virginia Fox Diamond with her devious plan to set up Foxy's – a fast-food joint by the river, using chicken carcasses from the humans' restaurants.'

Virginia Fox Diamond stood up and waved at her clapping fans.

'Not bad,' Thaddeus remarked. He made a mental note to have a chat with Virginia Fox Diamond after the competition was over.

'The third and, in my opinion, most inventive of our finalists are Thaddeus E. Fox and Snooty Bush with their devious plan to set up – wait for it – a *battery farm* here in the very heart of Cluckbridge, to supply us foxes with all the fresh chicken and eggs we can eat.'

There was a collective gasp from the assembled foxes. They stared at Thaddeus and Snooty Bush, open–mouthed.

'What's the matter?' Snooty Bush whispered nervously. 'Don't they like it?'

'On the contrary,' Thaddeus replied smugly, 'they love it. They just wish *they'd* thought of it first.'

A low muttering rippled round the room. All the foxes were talking at once. *A battery farm?! Chicken! Eggs! Chicken! Eggs! Chicken! Eggs! Fresh! Fresh! Fresh!* The noise rose into a crescendo as the foxes agreed what a brilliant plan it was.

The vixen in charge of proceedings clapped her paws together for silence. 'To judge who should be

the winner of tonight's competition I have great pleasure in introducing a very special guest. She is without doubt more devious and deadly to chickens than any fox . . .'

Thaddeus raised an eyebrow. *Not more devious and deadly than him, surely?*

'. . . and therefore uniquely placed to decide which of our three fantastic finalists should be given the support of the Society to put their plan into action. Please give a big welcome to the most venomous creature in the whole-wide world, Her Majesty, Cleopatra, the queen cobra!'

Thaddeus frowned. *Cleopatra, the queen cobra? Wasn't she the one who'd escaped from the City Zoo?* He'd read about it in a newspaper someone had thrown into Snooty's dustbin.

'She's still here?' Snooty Bush said, astonished. 'I heard she left Cluckbridge this morning on a boat to India.'

There was a deathly silence in the railway carriage as the queen cobra slithered along the bar. Thaddeus watched the foxes' reaction closely. They were

nervous. Cleopatra's surprise appearance had chilled the atmosphere by several degrees. She was obviously a villain to be reckoned with. He regarded her with interest as she raised her hood.

'Don't look at her!' Snooty Bush hissed at him. 'She'll hypnotise you. Everyone in the city knows that.'

All the other foxes were looking at their feet.

Thaddeus lowered his eyes. He didn't want to get hypnotised. Nor did he want to appear disrespectful to the world's most venomous snake. But he did want to get to know Cleopatra better. Something told him the two of them were going to hit it off.

'Sssssssome of you are sssssssurprised to sssssssee me,' Cleopatra began. 'You might have heard a rumour that I am currently on a boat bound for India.'

The foxes nodded their agreement, keeping their eyes low.

'That'sssssss what you are supposssssssed to think,' hissed Cleopatra. 'Sssssssso are the humansssssss. I made sure that one of them caught a glimpsssssssse of me on the quay.' She put her head to one side as if inviting a question.

'So how *did* you give everyone the slip, your majesty?' the vixen asked politely.

'I sssssslithered over the sssssssside of the ship and ssssssswam back to shore,' Cleopatra said. 'I wanted to stay and find sssssssomewhere dark and quiet to have my *babiessssssss*.'

Cleopatra was going to lay eggs? 'Congratulations, your majesty,' Thaddeus cried. He could feel the snake's eyes upon him.

'Who daresssssss to interrupt Cleopatra when she is ssssssspeaking?' the snake said, sharply.

'Thaddeus E. Fox,' he said, removing his top hat and bowing low. 'At your service, your majesty.'

'Ah,' Cleopatra hissed. 'One of our two prizewinnerssssssss.' She flicked her tongue in and out.

'You mean we won, your majesty?' Thaddeus E. Fox said, giving Snooty Bush a slap on the back.

'Yesssssss.' Cleopatra inclined her hood. 'Your plan is ingeniousssssss. You get first prize. In fact, it is ssssssso ingeniousssssss, I should like to help you.'

'What did you have in mind, your majesty?' Thaddeus asked.

'You ssssssssupply me with chicken and I will provide you with workers for your battery farm,' she said.

Workers? This was getting better and better. Thaddeus E. Fox hated working. 'Who did you have in mind, your majesty?'

'The ratsssssss.'

The foxes started muttering. The rats weren't popular in the city. They stole the foxes' food.

'But how will you get them to obey us?' Thaddeus asked. Rats could be difficult. They had opinions of their own. They also came in very large numbers, which could be troublesome to control.

'I will hypnotise them for you,' Cleopatra said.

Hypnotise them! Thaddeus felt a growing respect for the queen cobra. If Cleopatra hypnotised the rats, he could get them to do anything he wanted. He would have his very own rat army entirely at his disposal. The chickens of Cluckbridge wouldn't stand a chance.

'Sssssssssoooooo?' said Cleopatra. 'What do you sssssssay?'

'We should be delighted if you would join us, your majesty,' Thaddeus E. Fox said. 'Welcome to the team.'

Chapter Seven

The next day after breakfast at Aunt Mildred's, Amy stood outside the coop under the apple tree, her suitcase in one wing, feeling the wind in her feathers. She could hardly believe it. She was going home to Perrin's Farm at last.

'Bye, Amy! Bye! Have a good holiday!' Boo and Ruth each gave her a huge hug.

Amy squeezed them tight. 'Thanks, guys! Enjoy the party,' she said.

It had been agreed by everyone that the reports of Cleopatra's unexpected departure to India was indeed something to celebrate. As a result, Aunt Mildred and her friends were organising their first street party in ages.

The local rooster had been asked to crow the party invitation at the top of his voice at dawn tomorrow to all the chickens in the neighbourhood. Aunt Mildred and her friends were already busy sorting

out food and hats and crackers. Boo was rehearsing a gymnastics display, and Ruth was organising quizzes and games for the chicks, as well as being in charge of making sure that everyone got there and back safely without the foxes interfering. Luckily Ruth's self-packing suitcase had packed the mite blaster and several pepper pots by mistake, so if any of the foxes did try anything, she could give them a nasty dose of mites or a sneezing fit.

Amy was sorry to miss the party, but the holiday was only going to last for a few days, so she couldn't really afford to wait. She had decided to set off for home straight away.

Only one thing slightly troubled her. She hadn't actually told Professor Rooster she was going to see her parents instead of staying on at Aunt Mildred's, but Amy had persuaded herself he wouldn't mind. After all, she was only doing what she had originally planned before the Cleopatra mission started. She would tell him when they got back to Chicken HQ.

'See you next week!' Amy strapped on her flight-booster engine and waved goodbye to her friends.

59

She set the satellite navigation system on her super-spec headset to 'Perrin's Farm', pulled the goggles down over her eyes and soared into the sky.

Amy loved the feeling of flying. Like most chickens she could fly a bit by herself but it took a great deal of flapping and squawking before she got anywhere, and she couldn't go very high because her wings were too short and her tummy was too fluffy and seemed to attract more in the way of gravity than it should. But with the flight-booster engine, Amy could swoop and dive, like the albatross, as long as she didn't run out of fuel.

She glanced down. She could still see the patchwork of gardens. Ruth and Boo and the other chickens were tiny dots. She hoped they had a good time with Aunt Mildred. If anyone deserved a holiday it was Boo.

Her route took her along the river past old factories and dilapidated warehouses. Aunt Mildred had said that was where the foxes hung out. Amy could see why they would choose it: the warehouses looked dark and dingy, just the sort of place she could imagine foxes lurking. But after a while there were

no more buildings. Green and brown fields edged with thick hedges stretched away into the distance. Amy had reached the countryside. In half an hour she would be home.

Perrin's Farm looked just as she'd remembered it. There was the farmhouse, and the play barn where she

used to wrestle the goose, and the chicken coops in the yard. There was the dirt patch where the chickens had their dust baths and the grassy field where the horses grazed. There was the little school in the upturned water trough under the clump of bushes where she'd learned – well, not as much as she should.

And there were her friends, playing what looked like a really fun game of 'It'!

'Hey!' Amy landed with a bump.

The posse of chickens looked round. They blinked at her in surprise.

All of a sudden, Amy felt shy. It had been ages since she'd seen any of them. Maybe they wouldn't remember her.

'It's me, Amy!' she said, taking off her super-spec headset so they could see her properly.

'Amy?' said one of them. 'But your mum said you weren't coming!'

'Change of plan,' Amy explained. 'I decided I would in the end.'

'I'll go and tell your parents you're here,' another one offered. The chicken scurried off.

There was an awkward silence. Amy couldn't think of anything to say. The other chickens scuffed their feet on the ground.

'Did you really fly here?' asked a third chicken, eyeing Amy's equipment.

'Yes,' Amy said. She took off the flight-booster engine. 'Would you like a go?'

'Yes, please!' the chicken said.

Soon all the chickens were lining up to have a turn with the flight-booster engine.

'This is so cool!' they said, passing it from one to another.

Amy smiled bravely but inside she felt miserable. Her friends didn't seem at all interested in her or her new job – only the flight-booster engine. It was as if she had turned into a complete stranger.

'Watch out for the farmer,' a voice said. 'She might think it's a bit odd if she sees her chickens trying out a flying machine.' The voice belonged to a handsome cockerel. He held out his wings.

'Dad!' Amy cried. She raced up to him and threw her arms round him. 'And Mum!' she spotted her

mother emerging from one of the coops. She looked more tired than Amy recalled, but still very pretty in a rosy-cheeked, plump, chickeny way.

'Oh what a lovely surprise!' Her mum gave her a huge hug. 'Sorry if I kept you waiting. I'm incubating a clutch of eggs. I can't leave them for too long.'

So that was why her mother looked tired. She was broody!

'That's all right!' Oh, I'm so pleased to be home,' Amy said, hugging her back.

'We weren't expecting you,' her father said. 'We had a letter from Professor Rooster by pigeon post. He said you were on another mission.'

'It . . . finished,' Amy said vaguely. She didn't want to worry her parents with Cleopatra when she didn't have to, especially when her mother was expecting chicks.

'I'm longing to hear about your adventures,' her mother said. 'Come in and have some worm juice and a piece of seedcake.'

'See you later, guys!' Amy called to her friends. But they were too busy with the flight-booster engine to reply.

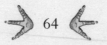

'Everything all right?' her father asked.

'Yes, great!' Amy said in what she hoped was a cheery voice. She followed her mother into the coop.

'Help yourself to seedcake,' her mother urged, settling back down on her nest. Amy caught a glimpse of several eggs peeping out from beneath her mother's cosy feathers. She counted seven in all: six brown and one white. Seven brothers and sisters! She wondered when they were due to hatch.

The seedcake was delicious. Amy washed it down with a cup of worm juice.

'Come on then,' her father said. 'Tell us all about it!'

So Amy did. She told her parents everything that had happened since she left Perrin's Farm for Tibet. She told them about the Kung Fu School for Poultry and meeting Boo and Ruth for the first time. She told them about Chicken HQ and Professor Rooster. She told them about Thaddeus E. Fox and the villains of the MOST WANTED Club. She even told them about James Pond, the annoying duck secret agent from Poultry Patrol, who kept barging in on the act

when the chickens didn't need him! The only bit she left out was Cleopatra. By the time she had finished it was dusk.

Her father whistled. 'Wow!' he said. 'You really have grown up.'

'Who'd have thought you'd do all that?' her mother said admiringly. 'It seems like only yesterday you were a chick.' She spread her feathers wider over her eggs.

Suddenly, for no apparent reason, Amy burst into tears.

'What's the matter?' her mother asked with concern.

'I don't know! I was so looking forward to coming home, and now I feel like I don't belong here any more,' Amy sobbed. 'I thought everything would be the same, and it isn't. At least, the farm is the same, and you're the same and my friends are the same but *I'm* different. I'm all grown up. No one wants to play with me. They're only interested in the flight-booster engine.'

Amy's mum and dad exchanged looks.

'Amy, it's not just you that's changed. Everyone has. Your friends have grown up too. Just in a different way from you,' her dad said.

'Have they? How?' Amy asked in a small voice.

'Well, most of them have started laying eggs for one,' her mother said.

Amy sighed. 'I haven't, I don't know how to do it. I've tried a few times and I really want to but nothing seems to happen.'

'It sounds like you've been too busy,' her mother said tactfully. 'Laying an egg's the sort of thing you need peace and quiet for. You can't do it when you're running about being a chicken warrior.'

'Maybe your friends can teach you,' her dad suggested.

'I can't ask *them*,' Amy said. 'I already told you, they're not interested in me.'

Her father gave a little cough. 'Have you stopped to think they might be worried that you're not interested in *them*?'

'Why would they think that?' Amy said, astonished.

'Well, you've been away and had adventures they

can only dream of,' her mother said. 'Maybe they think what they've been doing isn't very exciting in comparison.'

'But it is!' Amy protested. 'I'd love to lay eggs and play "It" and hang out in the barn and wrestle the goose. That's why I came back. I really missed all that.'

'Then tell them!' her father said.

'Okay,' Amy agreed. She could see that her parents were right. It wasn't just her who felt shy. She should give her friends another chance.

Just then there was a knock at the door.

Her mother went to answer it.

'Hello, Mrs Cluckbucket,' she heard one of her friends say, 'we brought Amy's flight-booster engine back.'

'Thank you,' Amy's mum said. 'Would you like to come in and see her?'

'No, it's okay. I expect she's busy . . .' A shuffling noise came from the doorway. It sounded to Amy as if her friends didn't really want to leave.

'Go on . . .' her father waved his wing at his daughter.

Amy leaped off the hay and scuttled to the door. 'Hey!' she said. 'I'm glad you're here.'

Her friends looked at her with hopeful expressions.

'I *am* busy – planning a midnight feast!' Amy announced, saying the first thing that came into her head. She hoped her parents wouldn't mind. 'Who wants to join?'

'We do!' her friends cried.

'We can have it at mine, if you like,' one of them offered. 'Seeing as your mum's – well, you know!'

Amy smiled gratefully.

'We could play games,' another one suggested.

'And tell spooky stories!' said a third.

'I can't wait. Oh, and by the way,' Amy said bravely, 'can anyone teach me how to lay an egg?'

Chapter Eight

In an abandoned warehouse beside the river, Thaddeus E. Fox stood on a crate under a bright, electric strip light. On separate crates either side of him were Snooty Bush and Cleopatra, the queen cobra. Thaddeus allowed himself a smirk. The warehouse was the perfect place to house an undercover battery farm.

According to Snooty Bush, the warehouse had once been used by humans as a flat-pack furniture store. Although it had been abandoned some years ago, it was still divided into sections by rows of floor-to-ceiling shelving units.

At the base of each row of shelves, a narrow conveyor belt fed towards a customer-collection area. Beyond the collection area were the checkout desks, and beyond the checkout desks stood the remains of a take-away burger grill.

Whoever it was that had designed the flat-pack furniture store, Thaddeus decided, could have had a

brilliant career in battery farming. As it was, they had set it up perfectly for the foxes.

Thaddeus and his cronies had congregated in the collection area, amongst piles of old cardboard boxes.

It was time to address the meeting.

'Huh, hum,' Thaddeus gave a little cough. The meeting came to order immediately with a respectful hush, not – Thaddeus recalled sourly – like the meetings of the MOST WANTED Club, whose members rarely paid sufficient attention to anything he had to say. His audience today looked much more promising.

The Society of Enterprising Foxes had assembled a team of a dozen of its best foxy brains to help set up the battery farm. Virginia Fox Diamond was amongst them. What a stroke of luck to find a warehouse with a burger grill, Thaddeus thought gleefully! The lovely Virginia was going to set up her fast-food restaurant, Foxy's, in it. He was sure it would be a hit.

In front of the foxes sat row upon row of rats. They all wore the same blank expression as if they had been brainwashed. That was because the rats *had* been brainwashed. Cleopatra had hypnotised every

single one of the revolting rodents into a robotic trance. They would do anything Thaddeus wanted.

'Welcome,' Thaddeus said, 'to the first meeting of the MOST ENTERPRISING Club of villains. The purpose of today's meeting is to unveil our devious plan for the City of Cluckbridge's first battery farm.'

His audience listened attentively.

Thaddeus flipped the title page over to the next sheet on the flipchart.

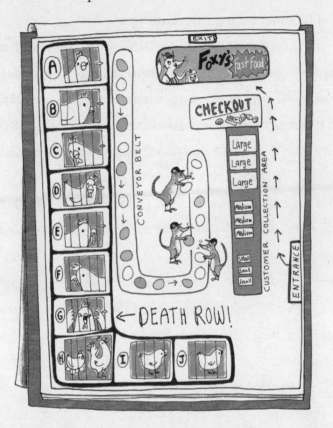

'The chickens will be kept in crates in rows A to F,' he said, pointing with his cane to the diagram. 'The first team of rats will collect the eggs and place them in containers, which will then be lowered onto

the conveyor belts beneath, to other members of the team. Are you with me so far?'

The rats nodded mechanically.

'The eggs will then travel along the conveyor belts to the customer-collection area where a second rat team will sort them into small, medium and large sizes for our customers to choose from.' He paused. Virginia Fox Diamond was watching him closely. She gave a little nod.

'Our customers will then proceed to the checkout where they will pay for their purchases.' He lavished a smile on Virginia. 'We'll accept most types of currency: clothes, jewellery, leather goods, bedding – anything they can steal from the humans. For a further fee they can then have their eggs fried at the burger grill by Virginia and her team of Fast Food Foxes.'

The foxes drooled.

'How soon can I offer chicken on the menu?' Virginia Fox Diamond demanded.

'Very soon,' Thaddeus replied calmly. He forgave the interruption. Virginia Fox Diamond was ambitious. He was beginning to think she might

be a suitable mate for himself. 'Let me explain the process,' he said. The best bit was still to come – the bit that *he'd* thought of, in fact, with a little help from Cleopatra. 'Once a chicken stops laying it will be taken to Row G – otherwise known as "death row".'

A murmur of approval at this part of the plan echoed around the warehouse.

Thaddeus waited for silence. 'Her majesty, Cleopatra, gets first pick of the chickens facing execution.' For one dreamy moment he imagined the queen cobra's jaws closing around Professor Rooster and his elite chicken squad. He shook himself. He must stay focused. 'After that, we all get a share.' He held his paw up for emphasis. 'Do not worry foxes; there will be plenty of chickens to go round.' He licked his lips. All this talk of chicken had left him feeling fiendishly hungry.

'How do we replenish our chicken supply?' asked Virginia.

'Row H will contain broody hens and a cockerel,' Thaddeus explained. 'These hens will be required to sit on their eggs until they hatch. Once hatched the chicks will be collected by the rats – NOT NIBBLED by the

way,' he added in a stern voice, 'and taken to rows I and J where they will be force fed a diet of chicken feed and GRO-BIG – an enlarging chemical – until they are old enough to lay eggs, thus replacing those chickens who have been removed from rows A to F to death row.'

'Where will we get the chicken feed and the GRO-BIG from?' Virginia persisted.

Gosh, she was good! Thaddeus flipped to the next diagram.

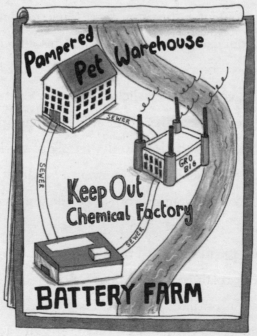

'The chicken feed will come from the Pampered Pet Warehouse, which is located here . . .' he pointed with his stick, 'and the GRO-BIG will come from the Keep Out Chemical Factory, which is located here. As you can see, the three buildings form a triangle. Fortunately for us they are connected by the same sewers which run underneath this area of the city. We need two more teams of rats whose job it will be to steal the goods. Any volunteers?' He looked hard at the rats.

The rats goggled back at him. 'We'll do it,' several rats said.

'Good. It should be straightforward to smuggle the supplies out at night.' Thaddeus gave a bow. 'And that, ladies and gentlemen, concludes our devious plan.'

He was rewarded with a dazzling smile from Virginia Fox Diamond. 'I'm impressed,' she said. 'Sounds like you've thought of just about everything.'

'Thank you,' said Thaddeus.

'There's just one small detail . . .'

'What's that?'

'How do we catch the chickens?'

Thaddeus's eyes gleamed. 'We're going to invite

77

them to your opening night.' He produced some
flyers from his pocket.

Opening tonight!

Dine in style at Cluckbridge's
newest chicken joint!

Games and Prizes!

chicken meal deals!

~~Cubs~~ chicks eat free!
Bring your friends and family!

~~Foxy's~~ Fiona's Fast Food Restaurant
The Abandoned Warehouse
By the river
Cluckbridge

Directions: take the nearest sewer.
Our friendly rat guides will be on
hand to help.

'You sure they'll fall for it?' Virginia asked doubtfully.

'Oh yes,' said Thaddeus, 'I'm sure.'

Chapter Nine

At his top-secret location near Chicken HQ, Professor Rooster was reading the *Cluckbridge Echo*. The newspaper had been brought to him that morning by one of his spies.

THE EVENING NEWS 50p

CLEOPATRA SEEN BOARDING BOAT TO MUMBAI: SNAKE DANGER BELIEVED TO HAVE PASSED

'Hmmm,' he said. 'I don't believe a word of it.' His first-hand experience of chicken predators over the years told him Cleopatra's supposed vanishing act was a trick. Snakes were like magicians: they could make you believe you had seen something when it was only an illusion. 'I'll bet she slipped off the boat and swam back to shore when everyone's back was turned,' he muttered. He hoped his elite chicken squad wouldn't fall for it. They needed to stay alert. It was two days since Cleopatra's escape from the zoo. She would be hungry again soon.

Just then something landed on the wooden roof of his hideout. He heard scratching and a faint coo.

A messenger pigeon! Perhaps it had important news.

The unseen bird tapped at the wood with its beak.

Tap-tap tap. Tappidy tap tap tap. Tap-a-tappity tap tap.

Professor Rooster listened carefully. The pigeon was tapping out code. It was the method his spies used to communicate with him.

Tap-tap tap. Tappidy tap tap tap. Tap-a-tappity tap tap.

Professor Rooster's face registered shock. Then anger. 'What?' he exclaimed. 'They've taken a holiday? Without asking *me*?!' Things were even worse than he had feared. If Boo, Ruth and Amy had been duped by Cleopatra into thinking they could take a break then the other chickens of Cluckbridge stood no chance against the cunning cobra. They would fall for anything. And meanwhile Boo and Ruth were off their guard and Amy wasn't even in the vicinity! She had gone to Perrin's Farm without telling him.

Professor Rooster felt betrayed. It was only a matter of time before Cleopatra struck, and his team – *his* elite chicken squad upon whom all the urban chickens were relying – would be caught napping. He shook his head crossly.

Yes, they were young, but the three of them should have learned by now that being a chicken warrior was all about discipline. It was about obeying instructions, not clearing off on holiday when you felt like it without checking with your boss first. This was Cleopatra they were talking about, for goodness

sake! She was a far more dangerous chicken predator than Thaddeus E. Fox and his MOST WANTED Club.

It was reckless. It was immature. It was downright stupid. Sometimes Professor Rooster thought his elite chicken squad just didn't have a clue!

Professor Rooster came to a decision. He needed a professional poultry protector. Somebirdy he could trust, someone who would be able to fly straight to Cluckbridge (via Perrin's Farm to collect Amy) and take charge of the operation before anybody got hurt. *Holidays, indeed!* He tapped a few keys on his laptop and spoke into the microphone.

'Hello,' he said, 'this is Rooster speaking. Is that Poultry Patrol?'

'Yes,' the polished voice of the receptionist replied. 'How can we help you this time, Professor?'

'Get me James Pond,' Professor Rooster said. 'I need to brief him on a mission.'

Chapter Ten

Back at Perrin's Farm Amy's first attempt at laying an egg had not been a success. After a great deal of coaching from her friends at the midnight feast (which had turned out to be loads of fun) and far too much toffee popcorn and worm juice, she had retired to the roosting box. At first she had found it difficult to sleep because of the toffee sugar rush. Then, when she did finally go to sleep she was restless because the popcorn gave her terrible indigestion. On several occasions during the night she had the uncomfortable sensation that she'd let rip with an enormous fart but when she woke up she found, to her amazement, that instead of passing wind she had actually laid an egg.

Of sorts.

The egg was a sorry looking thing. It was shaped a bit like a giant piece of toffee popcorn and had a knobbly shell, parts of which were as hard as a brick, and other parts of which were as soft as a marshmallow.

A small puncture in the membrane of one of the marshmallowy parts leaked egg yolk onto the straw. It only took a couple of sniffs to establish that the egg yolk smelled pungently of worm juice.

'Yuk,' said Amy, picking bits of yellow goo off her feathers.

'Let's have a look,' her mother said.

Amy shuffled over to let her mother see. 'I told you I couldn't do it,' she said despondently.

Her mother smiled. 'I don't think that's too bad, for a beginner.'

'But it's the wrong shape, and it smells funny,' Amy complained.

'That's because you ate too much toffee popcorn and drank too much worm juice before you went to bed,' her mother told her.

Amy was puzzled. 'What difference does that make?'

'It makes all the difference,' her mother said. 'What comes out one end depends on what goes in the other.'

Amy had no idea laying an egg was so complicated.

'For example,' her mother continued, 'if you eat lots of grit before you lay, the shell of your egg will be hard, like a brick. If, on the other hand, you don't eat ANY grit and drink lots of water, it will be very soft, like a marshmallow. If you eat toffee popcorn, it will be a bit of a mixture.'

'Oh,' said Amy. 'What about the inside?'

'Same thing,' said her mother. 'The flavour of the egg will depend on what you've eaten and drunk before you lay it. In this case, worm juice.' She waggled her wing at Amy. 'You need to have a balanced diet if you want to lay a decent egg, young lady.'

Amy wasn't very interested in laying a decent egg. She was more interested in laying peculiar ones. An idea for a game was forming in her little chicken brain. 'So, if I ate nettles,' she said slowly, 'would the egg yolk sting if it went in your eyes?'

'Probably.'

'What if I ate rotten vegetables?'

'Then you'd lay a stinky egg,' said her mother.

Amy grinned. She didn't feel despondent any more. Laying eggs could prove to be much more fun

than she had ever imagined. 'Thanks, Mum,' she said, collecting the eggy straw ready to throw it in the yard.

'What are you planning?' her mum said, seeing the mischievous look on Amy's face.

'Nothing!' Amy said innocently. That, of course, was a lie. But it wasn't a big whopper of a lie: it was a little fib, so, in Amy's eyes, it didn't really count. She was nearly grown up. Everyone said so. That meant her mum didn't need to know *everything* she got up to! She raced out of the coop and disposed of the yucky straw.

'Hey, guys! I've got the coolest idea for a game!' she hissed. She didn't want any of the other farm animals to hear.

The posse of young chickens gathered eagerly around Amy. She whispered her idea to her friends.

'You mean we have to eat something revolting?' one of them said.

'Yes,' said Amy. 'Or drink lots of water. Or eat lots of grit. Then we can make our eggs into bombs and drop them on the geese.'

Her friends giggled. It was a really good idea! The geese were always causing problems and had a nasty habit of bullying the chickens. In the old days Amy had sometimes got into trouble with her parents for wrestling with the geese and trying to teach them a lesson. But her idea about the egg bombs was way better. All her friends agreed.

'I'll make a brick bomb.' One of them started gobbling grit.

'I'll do a blobby egg.' Another one dunked its head in the water trough.

'I like Amy's idea about the nettles,' a third strutted over to the nettle patch and began to graze on the green leaves.

'What kind of egg bomb are you going to make, Amy?' asked another hen.

Amy tried to think of something really disgusting to flavour her egg bomb with. A cowpat would be good of course, or some horse manure, but she didn't think she could actually eat poo, however satisfying the end result. 'Flies,' she said eventually. 'If I swallow them whole, maybe they'll come out buzzing.'

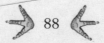

'Cool,' said her friend. 'I'll try ants.'

Amy ran around the farmyard with her mouth open, swallowing as many flies as she could. She hadn't had this much fun in ages. She was so happy to be home. Her friends hadn't forgotten her after all! Her dad had been right. Now that they knew Amy still wanted to play games and be friends, they did too. And this was the best game ever! She couldn't wait to see the look on those gooses' faces when the chickens started pelting them with egg bombs.

Just then the shadow of a bird passed overhead. Amy glanced up, fearing that it might be the albatross, come to take her back to Chicken HQ.

It wasn't the albatross. It was a large mallard duck. And it was wearing a bow tie.

'Bother-eggtion, no way!' Amy couldn't believe her bad luck.

The duck landed awkwardly in the farmyard. He dusted his feathers down and waddled towards Amy. 'The name's Pond,' he said, 'James Pond, duck sec agent.'

'I know!' Amy squawked. 'I've met you l

89

times before.' James Pond was an awful know-it-all show-off. He never missed an opportunity to boast. He also seemed to think he could boss her and Boo and Ruth around whenever he felt like showing up, uninvited, like now. 'What are you doing here anyway?' she asked.

'Professor Rooster sent me,' James Pond said ~ly.

·y's jaw dropped. *Professor Rooster? He knew she*

was here? But then of course he knew everything, just like Boo said. She should have realised he would find out she'd gone home. And now he was cross with her. That's why he'd sent James Pond.

'The professor suspects Cleopatra didn't go to India,' James Pond announced. 'He thinks she boarded the boat then swam back to shore when no one was looking. He's convinced she's still in Cluckbridge.'

Amy listened to James Pond with a sinking heart. She didn't know snakes could swim. And she had been so excited about going on holiday, she hadn't thought to question if the reports of Cleopatra's departure were true. She had just dashed off, leaving Boo and Ruth and Aunt Mildred. She had a horrible feeling she'd let them down.

'Professor Rooster has asked me to take charge of the mission because you guys suck,' James Pond concluded. 'Go and get your stuff. It's time to go to work.'

Amy didn't have the heart to argue any more. The street party was today. She just hoped they wouldn't be too late to warn Aunt Mildred. She scuttled off to bid her parents a hasty farewell.

'Something's come up,' she said as she threw everything into her suitcase and strapped on her flight-booster engine.

'Is it serious?' her mother asked anxiously.

'No,' Amy fibbed again. She felt terrible lying about something as important as this but she didn't want to worry her mum. The chicks were due any day. The news about Cleopatra could wait. She gave her mum and dad a hug. 'Just a training exercise – don't worry, I'll be back as soon as I can.'

Chapter Eleven

Aunt Mildred's coop was empty. Amy could see that the moment she flew over the garden. The coop had a forlorn air about it. There was no sign of the excited hustle and bustle of when she had left.

Amy landed inside the chicken wire after James Pond. She removed her super-spec headset and looked about for clues as to what might have happened. Boo's gymnastics equipment had been set up under the apple tree and then abandoned. A few discarded party hats and crackers lay on the ground. It looked as if the party had gone ahead as planned.

But then what? Had Cleopatra come?

Amy hopped up the steps to the coop. Inside everything was just as it had been when she had left. Except that there were no chickens – all of them including Boo and Ruth, had simply vanished.

Amy felt numb with shock. This was all her f
It was she who had suggested they take a h

They should have stayed on guard, just in case. She could see that now. No wonder Professor Rooster was cross.

'I'll go and check the other gardens,' James Pond poked his head round the coop door.

'Okay,' Amy replied dully. She watched him limber up, preparing to take off again. Then she turned her attention back to the coop. There must be a clue somewhere. She wished Boo and Ruth were here to help her. She was rubbish at being a chicken detective without the help of her two best friends.

A piece of paper lay face down on the floor. She picked it up and turned it over. Amy frowned. *That was strange!* It was an invitation to a party. Only it wasn't the street party Aunt Mildred had been organising. It was a different party altogether.

Opening tonight!

Dine in style at Cluckbridge's newest chicken joint!

Games and Prizes!

chicken meal deals!

~~Cubs~~ chicks eat free!

Bring your friends and family!

~~Foxy's~~ Fiona's Fast Food Restaurant
The Abandoned Warehouse
By the river
Cluckbridge

Directions: take the nearest sewer. Our friendly rat guides will be on hand to help.

Fiona's Fast-Food Restaurant? Was that where Aunt Mildred's friends had gone? Amy felt a sense of relief. Maybe their disappearance wasn't down to Cleopatra after all! If she and James Pond were quick they could warn them that the queen cobra was still in town.

She was about to go in search of James Pond when she heard a faint knocking beneath her feet. It was coming from the library. Quickly, her heart hammering in her chest, Amy brushed aside the straw and pulled up the hatch.

Two familiar eyes blinked at her from behind a pair of wire-rimmed spectacles.

'Ruth!' she cried.

Ruth clambered out from between the rows of books and took a long drink of water from the bowl. 'Phew,' she said, 'thank goodness you're here, Amy. I've been stuck down there for ages. I thought I was going to die of thirst. There's no way out from the inside.'

'What were you doing down there anyway?' asked Amy.

'Hiding.'

'Who from?'

'The rats.'

'The rats?' Amy stared at her blankly. 'I don't understand. Where's Boo? And Aunt Mildred?'

'The rats took them. They took everyone except me.'

Amy waved the invitation at her friend. 'But it says here . . .'

Ruth let out a big sigh. 'I know, I know. It says there that the rats are friendly. Well, don't believe a word of it, Amy – they're not. We were ambushed by them. The invitation was a trick. I'd better tell you what happened.'

The two chickens sat down. Amy listened patiently.

'After you left we got everything ready for the street party,' Ruth began. 'I must admit I was a bit nervous about escorting Aunt Mildred's friends here, just in case any foxes showed up . . .'

'How many chickens were there?' asked Amy.

'About fifty altogether,' Ruth said. 'But I had the mite blaster and the peppershakers, and Boo offered to help, so we made a start.'

'Is that when you were ambushed?' asked Amy.

Ruth shook her head. 'No. The rats were cleverer than that.'

'Go on,' said Amy.

'We'd got about half the chickens to Aunt Mildred's when we first saw them,' Boo said. 'They were in small groups, delivering flyers to the chicken coops.'

'You mean these?' Amy held up the invitation.

Ruth nodded. 'Yes. Well, when they saw what Boo and me were doing, they offered to help. They said when the street party was over they'd take us to Fiona's Fast-Food Restaurant for a worm burger. They said it was a really cool place and that they were sick of the foxes eating all their food. They said they wanted to make friends with us chickens which was why they volunteered to guide us through the sewers so that the foxes didn't get us.'

'Go on,' Amy said.

'It seemed fine at first,' Ruth said. 'We got everyone to Aunt Mildred's and had some food and played party games. The rats joined in. Then it was

time for Boo's gymnastics display. By then the rats were getting a bit restless. They kept asking when we'd be finished. They said they wanted to go to Fiona's before it got dark. That's when I started to get a bit suspicious. I mean, why would rats help chickens after all? Why not just go to Fiona's and take the food for themselves? We all know what they're like for stealing. So, anyway, I had the idea it might be a trick, that the rats might be working for someone else.'

'Cleopatra?' Amy suggested.

Ruth looked surprised. 'No. Why do you say that?'

'Professor Rooster thinks Cleopatra's still in Cluckbridge,' Amy said. 'That's why he sent James Pond to fetch me back from Perrin's Farm. That's why I'm here.'

Ruth scratched her head. 'Oh dear, this might be even worse than I thought.'

'What do you mean?' asked Amy.

Ruth pointed to the invitation. 'Did you notice anything familiar about it?'

'Not really,' Amy said.

'Well I did,' said Ruth. 'I thought I'd seen that handwriting before. So while Boo was finishing off the gymnastics display, I took the invitation inside the coop to have a good look at it with the magnifying glass.'

Amy nodded wisely. She wished she'd thought of the magnifying glass. It was something Professor Rooster sometimes put in the Emergency Chicken Pack for looking at clues. She didn't think she'd ever e a super brainy detective like Ruth.

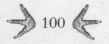

'Once I looked at it close up, I could see that it was written by an old enemy of ours . . .'

'Who?' asked Amy. She still didn't get it.

'Someone who makes it his job to trick unsuspecting chickens . . . someone who likes inviting chickens to dinners and putting them on the menu so that he and his cronies can eat them without the bother of having to catch them first . . .'

Suddenly Amy realised what Ruth was talking about: *Thaddeus E. Fox!* The invitation was his trademark. He was always inviting chickens to things and then trying to eat them. 'Thaddeus! You mean he's here? In Cluckbridge?'

'Looks like it,' Ruth said grimly. 'And now you've told me your news about Cleopatra, I wouldn't be surprised if he's teamed up with her.'

Cleopatra AND Thaddeus E. Fox?! Amy gave a little shudder. Dealing with one evil villain was bad enough, but dealing with two was impossible. 'What happened then?' she asked.

'I was just about to tell Boo about the invitation when I heard a commotion outside,' Ruth said. 'The

rats were rounding everyone up. They broke all Boo's gymnastic equipment and grabbed what was left of the food. Then they gnawed a hole in the chicken wire and started marching everyone out of the back gate towards the sewer. A group of them came to the coop to check round for any stragglers. That was when I hid in the library. I thought maybe I could tip off the professor and get word to you. It was only when I tried to lift the trap door that I realised I was, well, trapped.'

'We've got to get down to the river before it's too late,' Amy said.

Ruth grabbed the Emergency Chicken Pack. 'Should we go through the sewers?'

Amy shook her head. 'The rats might be down there. We'll use the flight-booster engines. Let's get Pond. We can fill him in on the way.'

Chapter Twelve

At the warehouse, egg production was already in full swing.

'What a stroke of luck to find so many chickens in one place!' Snooty Bush rejoiced.

'Indeed, Snooty!' Thaddeus E. Fox agreed. 'I couldn't have planned it better myself!' The pair of foxes walked up and down the rows of shelving units, grinning from ear to ear. The battery farm had got off to a flying start.

The crates in rows A and B were already bulging with the chickens from the raid at Aunt Mildred's. Meanwhile the crates in rows C, D, E and F were rapidly filling up with chickens from other parts of the city who had seen Thaddeus's flyer for Fiona's Fast-Food Restaurant and flocked to their local sewer, only to find themselves ambushed by rats and frog-marched to captivity.

Business was brisk. A queue of foxes was waiting

at the checkouts. A second queue of foxes had formed at Virginia's burger grill to get their eggs fried. Thaddeus and Snooty were on their way to making a killing.

The two devious foxes rounded the corner to rows I and J. A few broody hens sat on clutches of eggs. They looked dazed and miserable. 'How long until they hatch?' Snooty Bush asked the rat foreman in charge.

'A few days,' said the rat.

'Have you laced the feed with GRO-BIG?' Thaddeus barked.

'Yes, sir,' the rat said.

'Good. As soon as the chicks hatch, stuff them full of it to get them ready for laying,' Thaddeus ordered, 'or for eating if they're roosters. We don't need any more of them.'

'Yes, sir.'

'Are *all* the hens laying by the way?' Snooty Bush asked.

'All except one, sir. We've already moved her to Row G.' The rat gave the foxes a knowing look.

'Is she old and scrawny?' Thaddeus asked.

'No, sir. She's plump and juicy, but she can't lay an egg to save her life.'

'How curious,' Thaddeus said. 'Let's have a look at her.'

'Right you are, sir.' The rat led the way around the corner to death row.

A plump chicken with beautiful honey-coloured feathers sat forlornly on a thin bed of straw in an otherwise empty cage. A bowl of feed beside her remained untouched.

'Well, well, well . . .' Thaddeus's face split into a delighted grin. 'Will you look at what the rats brought in?'

'What is it, Thaddeus?' Snooty Bush asked him. 'Do you know that chicken?'

'That, my dear Snooty, is one of Professor Rooster's elite chicken squad.' He addressed the chicken. 'Where are your two friends?'

Boo cowered in the corner of the cage. 'They're not here,' she said.

'I can see that,' Thaddeus snarled. 'Where are they?'

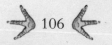

'On holiday,' Boo said.

'Where?'

Boo said nothing.

'Tell me where,' Thaddeus growled, 'or I'll feed you alive to Cleopatra. Ah,' he said, seeing the look of terror in Boo's eyes, 'I can see you've already heard of our new business partner. Well? Where are the other two?'

'Promise you'll let me go back to the other cage if I tell you?' Boo whispered.

Thaddeus drew himself up and gave Boo a little bow. 'You have my word as an old Eat'emian.'

'I don't know where Ruth is,' Boo said. 'She was at the party but she disappeared.'

Snooty Bush gestured to the lines of chickens. 'She may be with the others.'

Thaddeus narrowed his eyes. 'I'll find her if she is. What about the little fat one? The one with the wrestling moves?' he demanded.

Boo looked at him stubbornly.

'Spit it out,' Thaddeus said, 'or I'll take you to Cleopatra.'

'Amy went to Perrin's Farm to stay with her parents. She doesn't know anything about this. Just leave her alone.' Boo hid her face in her wings and started to sob.

Thaddeus regarded her with contempt. 'Where's Perrin's Farm?' he asked, turning to Snooty Bush.

'I'm not sure. Somewhere near Cluckbridge, I think,' Snooty Bush replied.

'We'll check the map,' Thaddeus E. Fox leered at Boo. The rat was right — she *was* very plump and juicy-looking but he had already decided he wasn't going to eat her. He was going to watch Cleopatra do it. Being ingested by the queen cobra would take far longer and be much more painful than a quick snap of *his* jaws. It was the perfect revenge for all the humiliation he had suffered at the wings of Professor Rooster and his elite chicken squad.

'Are you going to take me back to the other cage now?' Boo asked.

'No,' Thaddeus said unpleasantly. 'You're staying here until Cleopatra sends for you.'

Boo gasped. 'But you promised!' she said.

Thaddeus grinned. 'Let me give you a word of advice. Never trust an old Eatemian! We're all vagabonds and crooks! I thought you'd have realised that by now.'

Boo threw herself onto the straw in despair.

'Enjoy your last meal,' Thaddeus chuckled.

'Thaddeus!' Virginia Fox Diamond came loping towards them. 'There you are.' Thaddeus straightened his waistcoat. 'What can I do for you, Virginia?' he asked in his most charming voice.

'We need more eggs,' said the vixen. 'We're not keeping up with demand.'

'But we've only just started production,' Snooty Bush protested.

Virginia Fox Diamond ignored him. 'There aren't enough eggs. And there's no chicken. My customers don't want to wait. We need to feed them before they get tired of the queues and start going elsewhere.' She prowled about in frustration.

'There are more chickens on the way,' Thaddeus objected. 'The rats are still giving out the flyers.'

Virginia Fox Diamond shook her head impatiently.

'I've done my sums, Thaddeus. The battery farm is a brilliant idea, but there aren't enough chickens in Cluckbridge to feed all the foxes who are coming here. We need to think bigger.'

'Bigger?' Thaddeus echoed. 'What have you got in mind?'

'It's hush hush,' Virginia Fox Diamond gave the rat foreman a filthy look. The rat scuttled off. Virginia beckoned the two foxes away from Boo's cage and whispered her plan into their furry ears.

A look of surprise came over Thaddeus. It was followed by an expression of wonder, as if Virginia had thrown him a surprise party in a hen house.

'So what do you think?' said Virginia, stepping back.

'I think it's the most brilliant idea I've ever heard in my life,' Thaddeus replied. And he meant it. 'Let's go and tell Cleopatra. We were on our way to see her anyway.'

'I'll get the flipchart,' Snooty Bush offered.

The three foxes moved away, laughing.

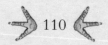

'Psssst!'

Boo lifted her head. The voice came from somewhere above her, along with a faint droning, like an engine.

'Psssst!' said another voice.

All at once two familiar-looking chickens wearing flight-booster engines landed on the shelf beside the cage.

'Amy! Ruth! It's you!' Boo rejoiced.

Amy removed her super-spec headset. 'Hello Boo! Sorry we took so long.'

Ruth produced Aunt Mildred's pliers from her backpack. 'Don't worry, Boo, we'll have you out of there in a jiffy.'

'Let me.' Amy took the pliers from Ruth. She cut a neat hole in the wire with her strong wings. Boo wriggled out. 'Are you all right?' Amy asked her.

'Just about,' said Boo. She gave her friends a huge hug. 'Did you see what happened?'

Amy nodded. 'Most of it. We got here just when

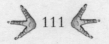

Thaddeus and Snooty Bush started giving you a hard time. I wanted to give Thaddeus a big punch in the snout but James Pond told me not to. He said we had to wait until they'd gone.'

'James Pond?' Boo said. 'What's he doing here?'

Amy sighed. 'Professor Rooster sent James Pond to collect me from Perrin's Farm. The professor was cross with me. He said I shouldn't have gone on holiday without his permission. He's put James Pond in charge.' She glanced around the battery farm. 'I can't blame him, though. He was right. I should never have gone home. This place is awful.'

Boo looked ashamed. 'I'm sorry I told Thaddeus where you were, Amy. I hope I haven't put *your* family in danger.'

'It's all right,' Amy said gently. 'It's not your fault Thaddeus is such a beast. I'm sure I'd have done the same if he'd threatened to feed *me* to Cleopatra.'

Boo frowned. 'What about that vixen though? She said there weren't enough chickens in Cluckbridge to feed all the foxes. It sounded as though she wanted to get hens from other places as well.'

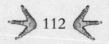

'I don't see how she's going to do that,' said Amy. 'Don't worry about it, Boo. The most important thing is to get everyone out of here alive.' She offered Boo her flight-booster engine. 'Now put this on before the rats come back. We need to make a plan. We've got some chickens to rescue!'

Chapter Thirteen

The three chickens sat in the loft of the warehouse with James Pond.

'We should get all the chickens back to Aunt Mildred's,' Boo said. 'They'll be safe there until the humans return them to their owners. We'll make a break for it when the warehouse closes for the night.'

'What about the rats?' asked Ruth. 'The foxes might leave them on guard.'

'I've got something to deal with them.' James Pond produced a packet of grated cheese from a holster under his wing.

'Sleepy Cheese,' Amy read. 'What does that do?'

'Duh!' said James Pond. 'The clue is in the name – it knocks them out, that's why it's called Sleepy Cheese.'

Amy regarded him with dislike. Okay, maybe she should have guessed what Sleepy Cheese did, but there was no need to be so rude. She only had a small brain and part of it was still busy thinking

over what Virginia Fox Diamond and Thaddeus had been plotting. If Virginia wanted more chickens, the obvious place to get them was from the local farms. But most farmers hated foxes. They were good at keeping them out.

'Amy, pay attention!' James Pond was still going through the plan. 'When the battery farm closes, we scatter the Sleepy Cheese. Once the rats are asleep, we let the captives out, then you three lead them back through the sewer to Aunt Mildred's.'

'Eerrrgghhh,' said Amy, 'I'm not doing that. My feathers will get poo-ey.'

'That's an order.' James Pond quacked.

'We'd better do it, Amy, or Professor Rooster might not let us stay on as chicken agents after this mission,' Ruth whispered.

Amy glowered at James Pond. It was typical of him not to get his feathers dirty.

'What happens if we meet any rats in the sewer?' Boo asked.

'You can use the Stuff-a-Snake,' James Pond said.

'What's that?' asked Amy.

'It's a replica of Cleopatra made out of an old cobra skin. All you need to do is blow it up with the pump, like a balloon. The rats will think it's really her. They'll run away, I guarantee it.' James Pond gave Ruth the equipment. She put it in her backpack.

'What are you going to do while we're doing all that?' Amy asked crossly.

'Capture Cleopatra and return her to the City Zoo before she lays her eggs,' James Pond said.

'How?' Amy demanded. It was equally typical of James Pond to claim all the glory.

'With this.' James Pond produced a flat oblong packet from the holster.

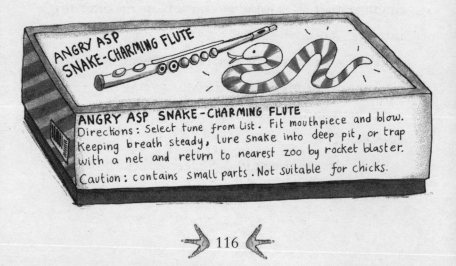

ANGRY ASP SNAKE-CHARMING FLUTE

ANGRY ASP SNAKE-CHARMING FLUTE
Directions: Select tune from list. Fit mouthpiece and blow. Keeping breath steady, lure snake into deep pit, or trap with a net and return to nearest zoo by rocket blaster.
Caution: contains small parts. Not suitable for chicks.

'That's so cool,' said Ruth, examining the gadget. 'Where did you get all this stuff from?'

'The Emergency Chicken Pack,' James Pond said. 'The Professor told me to take whatever I needed. There's a net and a rocket blaster as well.'

Amy's cheeks went bright red. *Now he was stealing their gadgets!*

Ruth sighed. 'I wish I could invent something as good as that.'

'You did,' Amy said. 'You invented the self-packing suitcase.'

James Pond gave the chickens a withering look. 'Get real, you two. A self-packing suitcase isn't going to defeat a queen cobra.'

'It might if she swallowed something metal,' Amy retorted.

'The only thing she's going to swallow, if you don't shut up, is chicken,' said James Pond.

'What tunes does the snake–charming flute play?' Boo asked.

'Yeah. How do you know Cleopatra will like any of them?' Amy said.

James Pond gave her a dirty look. 'Let's see.' He read down the list.

Snake, rattle and roll
Hiss me baby, one more time
Cobra Cobana
Fang you for the Music
In the jungle, the mighty jungle, the cobra sleeps tonight
We're all going to the zoo tomorrow

'Maybe not the last one,' James Pond said. 'I'll go for *In the Jungle*. It's nice and soothing. It'll make Cleopatra think of home.'

'How are you going to get her back to the zoo once you've charmed her?' Amy asked sulkily. It seemed like James Pond had all the answers.

'Once I've lured her into the net with the snake-charming flute, I'll attach it to the rocket blaster, tap in the coordinates of the City Zoo and press the green button. BOOM. And off she goes.'

'What about Thaddeus? And Snooty Bush and all the other foxes?' Boo asked.

'They'll be tucked up in their beds,' James Pond said. 'Cleopatra doesn't want company right now. All she wants is somewhere dark and quiet to lay her eggs. She'll be here alone. And by the time the foxes realise what's happened it will be too late.'

'Where do you think she's hiding?' asked Ruth.

'In the cellars.'

'How can you be so sure?' Amy wondered.

'I used my vibrating snake detector,' James Pond said. 'The closer you get, the more it vibrates. It was nearly off the scale when I got to the cellar door.'

'Was that in the Emergency Chicken Pack too?' asked Ruth.

'No, it's standard Poultry Patrol issue,' James Pond boasted. 'Pretty cool, huh?' He smoothed his bow tie, ready for action. 'Any more questions?'

Amy couldn't think of any. James Pond's plan was a good one even if it did mean him stealing all their gadgets. If it worked they probably wouldn't have to worry about Virginia Fox Diamond and Thaddeus any more. Without Cleopatra egging them on the city foxes would give up and go back to raiding dustbins

119

and fighting the rats; Virginia Fox Diamond would stop frying eggs in her Foxy's Fast-Food Restaurant; Thaddeus would return to the burrow in the Deep Dark Woods with his tail between his legs, and they would go back to Chicken HQ until their next mission. She might even get to go home to finish her holiday if Professor Rooster gave her permission.

If it worked . . .

Something niggled at Amy's little chicken brain: something she felt she ought to tell James Pond; something the professor had said before they left; something about Cleopatra. The problem was her brain was so crowded with other things like Sleepy Cheese and what Virginia Fox Diamond was up to and the thought of her feathers getting covered in poo in the dirty sewers that she couldn't remember what it was for the life of her. *Perhaps she'd just got a small worm stuck between her ears.*

Amy shrugged. 'Okay,' she agreed. 'You win. Let's do it.'

Chapter Fourteen

An hour later the battery farm finally closed for the night and all the foxes went home. The last three foxes to leave were Thaddeus, Snooty Bush and Virginia Fox Diamond. They emerged from a door beside Row A – the door to the cellar – and headed for the exit. The rescuers watched them say goodnight to one another. They slunk out into the night, leaving the rats on guard.

'Looks like James Pond was right about the cellar,' Boo said. 'Cleopatra must be down there.'

'What on earth have they been talking to her about all this time?' Ruth wondered. 'I thought Cleopatra wanted peace and quiet.'

Amy was wondering that too. It had to do with Virginia Fox Diamond's plan to get more chickens, she was sure of that, but there wasn't time to think any more about it now.

'Boo, you spread the Sleepy Cheese,' James Pond

ordered. 'Amy and Ruth, you let everyone out of the cages. I'll take Cleopatra. Ready?'

The three chickens nodded.

'Good luck,' said James Pond. He levered himself out of the loft and waddled along the rafters towards Row A.

The others waited until he was out of sight.

'Your turn, Boo,' Ruth said.

Amy watched as Boo took off and flew as low as she dared up and down between the rows of battery hens, scattering Sleepy Cheese. The army of rat guards stopped what they were doing and scurried towards the flakes of cheese. A horrible snuffling noise ensued as the rats gobbled it down. Very soon they lay flat on their backs, snoring.

'Good work!' Ruth said. 'Now it's down to us, Amy.'

Amy checked her flight-booster engine was securely fastened and followed her friend out of the loft. Up and down the rows of cages they went, freeing the imprisoned chickens. They worked as a team. Amy opened the cages with Aunt Mildred's

pliers, and Ruth ushered the chickens safely to the warehouse floor. Boo joined them. 'What can I do?' she asked.

'Keep them together,' Ruth said in her sensible, teacher's voice. 'Tell them to stay calm. Make sure they don't panic.'

'Okay.' Boo flew down to the flock of scared chickens. 'It's all right. We're going to get you home,' she said.

Amy's heart filled with pride. No wonder Boo's skill was perseverance. Even though she had been through a terrible ordeal on death row, she still had the determination to help others.

The next cage they came to contained Aunt Mildred.

'Amy!' she cried. 'And Ruth! Goodness, am I pleased to see you!' Her face took on an anxious expression. 'Where's Boo? Is she all right?'

'Yes,' Ruth affirmed. 'She's fine. She's looking after the chickens on the ground.'

'I can help her with that,' Aunt Mildred said. She fluttered down to join her niece.

It took a long time to empty all the cages – a lot longer than Amy had expected – but eventually they finished. She stretched her sore wings. She had blisters from where she had gripped the pliers. 'Let's get them to the sewer,' she said, landing beside Boo.

An alarmed squawking from the assembled flock greeted this suggestion. None of them wanted to go back there!

'Everything will be okay, I promise,' Boo said soothingly.

'It's our best chance – please, do as Boo says,' said Aunt Mildred.

The chickens signalled their agreement with soft clucking.

Boo led the way out of the factory. The chickens flocked after her, Ruth and Aunt Mildred bringing up the rear.

Amy hovered about, trying to keep the flock together. They couldn't afford any stragglers. The night was very dark. If a chicken got lost it would be almost impossible to find it.

'Here!' Boo had reached the sewer. She heaved at the grate with her strong wings.

'Let me help.' Amy grasped the metal bars. She groaned.

'What's wrong, Amy?' Boo asked.

'Just a couple of blisters,' Amy said. 'It's nothing.'

The two chickens dug their heels into the dirt and pulled with all their might. The grate came away with a metallic grinding.

 125

Ruth hurried up to them with the Stuff-a-Snake. She gave it to Amy. 'I'd better stay at the back with Aunt Mildred and make sure we don't lose anyone. Are you okay to blow this up if we see any rats?'

Amy nodded. 'Do you think James Pond is okay?' The niggling in her brain had started up again. She felt really worried about the duck. 'He's taking ages to capture Cleopatra. I thought he'd have got her out of the cellar and sent her back to the zoo by now.'

'I'm sure he's fine,' Ruth said. 'He had it all worked out. He's probably just being careful. And he had to find her first, don't forget. The cellars probably run all the way under the warehouse.'

'I suppose,' Amy said. She turned her attention back to the job in hand.

Boo hung back from the edge of the sewer.

'I'll go first,' Amy said bravely. She pulled her super-spec headset over her eyes and turned the setting to NIGHT VISION. It would be even darker in the sewers and chickens couldn't see in the dark unless they had special equipment like she, Boo and Ruth did. 'Tell the chickens to get in a line,' she said.

'Get them to keep one wing on the hen in front. That way no one gets separated.'

'Okay.'

Amy lowered herself over the edge. She heard water trickling beneath her. There was a terrible smell of poo. But there was nothing else for it. She took a big gulp of fresh air and dropped down into the sewer.

SPLASH!

Amy felt for the bottom of the tunnel with her toes. The water wasn't very deep and she found she could easily stand up. Ignoring the sticky blobs of brown bobbing beside her, she paddled along the sewer to make room for the other hens. She heard splashing behind her as one after another the flock of frightened chickens followed her lead.

SPLOSH. SPLOSH. SPLOSH.

Amy trudged along. The chickens trudged behind her in a line.

SPLISH. SPLISH. SPLISH. SPLISH. SPLISH. SPLISH. SPLISH.

Wait a minute! What was that? It sounded like

something ahead of her was doing an energetic front
crawl.

Boo was beside her. 'It's the rats,' she whispered.
'They can swim. You'd better get the Stuff-a-Snake.'
She halted the line of chickens.

Amy took the Stuff-A-Snake out of her backpack.
She inserted the pump into the nozzle and began to
force the air through the pump. James Pond was right.

It was like blowing up a gigantic balloon. Gradually the pretend cobra began to inflate. Backwards and forwards went Amy's wings until her shoulders were as sore as her blisters. The last part of the Stuff-a-Snake to inflate was the cobra's head.

BOOMPH! Up it went, the hood towering above the dirty water. It was just as well the other chickens couldn't see it, Amy thought, or they would all die of fright.

The splishing stopped immediately. It was replaced by an eerie silence, punctuated by the occasional squeak.

'Why don't they run away?' asked Boo. 'James Pond said they would.'

'I'm not sure,' said Amy. It was almost as if the rats were too scared to move. 'Stay here.' She turned her super-spec headset to TURBO VIEW so that she could see better and took a few, tentative steps. She started. There were dozens of rats floating about. Their eyes were open and staring. But they weren't staring at her. They were staring at the face of the Stuff-a-Snake. And they didn't look scared, exactly – more glazed over . . .

'They've been hypnotised by the Stuff-a-Snake!' Boo said.

Hypnotised! Professor Rooster's warning came flooding back to Amy.

Whatever you do, don't make eye contact with Cleopatra or she'll hypnotise you.

Amy gasped. That's what had been niggling away in her little chicken brain. It wasn't a worm at all. It was Professor Rooster's warning.

'James Pond's in trouble,' she said.

'What? How do you know?' said Boo.

Amy tried to stay calm. 'James Pond thought the rats would run away when they saw the Stuff-a-Snake,' she explained. 'That means he doesn't know what happens if you look into Cleopatra's eyes.'

'You mean she'll hypnotise *him*?'

'Yes.'

'But Cleopatra won't know he's there if it's dark,' Boo said. 'He'll creep up on her. By the time she hears the snake-charming flute it will be too late for her to do anything about it.'

'No, you're wrong.' The second part of the

professor's warning echoed around Amy's little brain. *And watch out for her tongue. That's how she senses things if she can't see them.* 'Don't you remember, it's not just her eyes Professor Rooster told us to watch out for, it's her tongue. She'll sense him with it, especially if he's wearing the vibrating snake detector.'

'I'll come with you,' Boo said at once.

'No,' Amy said. 'You get the chickens to safety. I'll be all right. My special skill is courage, after all.'

'Okay.' Boo gave her a big hug.

Amy sploshed back along the line of chickens.

'What's happened?' Ruth asked in a low voice.

Amy took her to one side and explained.

'I should have thought of that! I'm supposed to be the intelligent one,' Ruth said ruefully.

Amy shook her head. 'It was only when I saw the rats' faces I remembered what the professor told us.'

Ruth looked thoughtful. 'One good thing is, if the rats are hypnotised, they'll do anything we tell them.'

'Like what?'

'Well, they can show us the way back to Aunt

Mildred's for a start. The sat nav on the super-spec headsets doesn't work properly underground. I was worried we might get lost.'

That was something, Amy thought. The sewers probably led in all sorts of directions right under the city. It would be easy to get lost without the sat nav unless the rats showed them the way.

'Here!' Ruth took the Emergency Chicken Pack from her backpack and gave it to Amy. 'I don't know what's left in it, or whether it will be any use, but you'd better have it, just in case.'

The two chickens hugged.

'We'll come back for you, just as soon as we get everyone to safety,' Ruth said.

'Okay,' Amy said, as bravely as she could. She hoped there'd be something of her to come back *for*. Then she paddled off through the stinking water back to the grate.

Chapter Fifteen

After the dank sewer, it was almost a relief to be back in the warehouse. Amy gave her feathers a quick wash under the tap in the grill kitchen and dried them on one of Virginia Fox Diamond's best tea towels. She threw it down beside Virginia's burger grill and went in search of James Pond.

The rats were still sleeping. Amy crept past them. She wasn't sure how long the Sleepy Cheese would last and she didn't want to wake them up. At the door to the cellar she stopped. James Pond's footprints were visible on the dirty floor. Amy knelt down to get a closer look. The footprints only led *towards* the door, not away from it. That meant James Pond was still down there.

She hesitated. If James Pond hadn't already captured Cleopatra then *she* would have to try. Maybe now was a good time to check out the remaining contents of the Emergency Chicken Pack. Professor

Rooster always put useful things in it to help the chickens complete their missions. The problem was: a) James Pond had already helped himself to the best stuff; and b) it was usually Ruth who worked out what the gadgets were for. Even so, there might be something in there that would hold Cleopatra while she found out what had happened to James Pond. It was worth a try.

She held up the pack and shook it. Several objects tumbled out. She examined them carefully. The first one was a packet of burp powder. The second one was something called a Venombrella. The third one was a large stack of padded egg boxes addressed to the City Zoo, and the fourth one was a mirror.

Amy scratched her head, trying to work out what each one was for. The egg boxes were easy, anyway. They must be to send the snake eggs back to the zoo if Cleopatra laid them before they captured her. And the mirror must be so that you could see Cleopatra without looking her in the eye and getting hypnotised. That left the Venombrella and the Burp Powder.

She examined the Venombrella. It looked exactly like a chicken-sized folded-up umbrella. It had a metal handle and a button to put it up. Amy peered at the label.

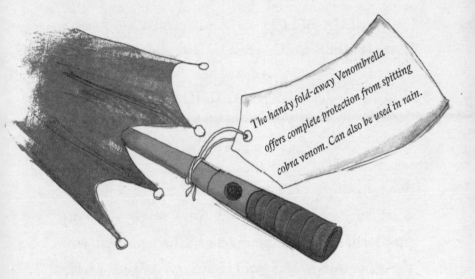

The handy fold-away Venombrella offers complete protection from spitting cobra venom. Can also be used in rain.

Cobra venom! *Of course!* The Venombrella would keep her safe from Cleopatra's poison. *Now for the burp powder.* Maybe there was a clue about that on the label too?

BURT'S BURP POWDER

NOT SATISFIED WITH THE QUALITY OF YOUR BURPS?
WANT TO OUT-BELCH YOUR FRIENDS? THEN BURT'S
BURP POWDER IS FOR YOU

DIRECTIONS:

For a MEGA-BELCH take one dose of Burt's Burp Powder

For a SUPER MEGA-BELCH take two doses of Burt's
Burp Powder

To produce a TOXIC VOLCANIC ERUPTION the
whole packet may be consumed

Note: Risk of vomiting if taken after food

What good would that do? Amy threw the burp powder back in the Emergency Chicken Pack with the other things. She would have to ask Ruth what it was for. *If* she got the chance, that was.

Amy creaked the cellar door open and hopped down the stairs. She felt a chill run through her feathers. Cleopatra could be anywhere.

'Sssssssoooooooo,' said a soft voice, 'what have we here?'

Amy froze.

'It ssssssseeems I have a sssssssecond visitor,' said the voice. 'I could ssssssssmell you from outside the door!'

Darn it, thought Amy. It was all that poo from the sewers.

'Turn on the lightsssssss, James, sssssssso that she can sssssssee me better.'

Light flooded the cellar. Amy was taken unawares. She was still wearing her super-spec headset so that she could see in the dark. Now she couldn't see anything! She tried to pull it off.

'Jamessssssss, help her with those, would you?'

Amy felt a pair of strong wings tug at the super-spec headset.

Amy's little chicken brain began to register that something was wrong. Why would Cleopatra ask James Pond to turn the lights on and help her out of her headset? And why would James Pond do what the queen cobra told him? *Because he had been hypnotised, that's why!*

'Yes, your majesty,' James Pond said. His voice was flat and toneless.

'Wake up, you idiot!' Amy yelled at him.

 137

James Pond didn't seem to hear her. The super-spec headset came off with a final tug.

'That'ssssssss better . . .'

Amy caught a glimpse of a long, dark brown coil of thick rope. Only it wasn't rope, it was Cleopatra. The snake was drawing herself up. 'Look into my eyessssssss,' she said, 'you know you want to.'

'No I don't!' Amy risked a look at James Pond instead. *His* eyes were like saucers. They were fixed on Cleopatra, like the rats in the sewer when they saw the Stuff-a-Snake.

'Hold her, James,' Cleopatra ordered.

Amy struggled as James Pond gripped her round the tummy. She closed her eyes against the queen cobra. *She mustn't look into her eyes. She mustn't!* 'Get off me, you dopey duck!' she shouted.

'Shan't,' James Pond replied.

For goodness sake! She'd have to use one of her wrestling moves on him. James Pond was about the same size as some of the geese at Perrin's Farm: the goose-slammer would do. Amy reached back and grabbed James Pond round the neck. Then she pulled him right over her head. He landed on his back and let out a groan as his head met the floor. *Oh no!* She'd knocked him out! She wondered what James Pond had done with the rest of the snake-catching equipment. Now she wouldn't get the chance to ask him.

Chapter Sixteen

'It'ssssssss Amy, isssssssn't it?' Cleopatra was swaying above her, still trying to make eye contact. Amy whipped round so that her back was to the snake and rummaged in the Emergency Chicken Pack. Her wing closed on the object she wanted. She pulled the mirror out of the pack and held it up. Now she wouldn't have to look Cleopatra in the eye. She could look at her reflection instead.

She adjusted the angle on the mirror. Cleopatra's face came into view.

Amy quivered with fright. 'How do you know my name?'

'Oh, I know all about you,' Cleopatra hissed. 'And your friendsssssss, Boo and Ruth. In fact, there'sssssss nothing I don't know. James was kind enough to fill me in on every detail. I know where you live. I know about Chicken HQ. I know about Professor Roosssssssster. I even know about your dispute with Thaddeusssssss.'

Amy was horrified.

'Use your mirror if you want,' said Cleopatra with contempt. 'Nothing will sssssssave you. But we can have a little chat before sssssssssupper if you like. It will whet my appetite.' There was a pause. 'It was hungry work laying my eggs.'

Amy gasped. 'You've laid them already?'

'Yesssssss,' said Cleopatra proudly. 'I laid them yesssssssterday.'

'Where are they then?' Amy changed the angle on the mirror again. More of Cleopatra's coils came into view. She was sitting on a nest of straw. But there was no sign of any eggs.

'Try and guesssssssssssssssssss,' suggested Cleopatra playfully.

Amy couldn't think what she meant. *Maybe the eggs were elsewhere in the cellar. Maybe she hadn't laid them at all. The queen cobra could be bluffing.*

'You know the battery farm's finished?' Amy said, stalling for time. 'The chickens are safe. Boo and Ruth have taken them back to Aunt Mildred's.'

'But it'sssssss not finished,' Cleopatra replied.

'It'ssssss only just started thanks to Virginia. She's a bright girl: she'd make a good ssssssssnake.'

Virginia? Amy's mind went back to the whispered conversation between the foxes. 'What are you talking about?'

'Virginia wants to exsssssssspand production outside the city,' Cleopatra said. 'She ssssssssuggested we begin operations at some of the local farms.'

The farms! So she had guessed right about that. 'How can you?' Amy said. 'The farmers will kill the foxes if they see them anywhere near the chicken coops. Even Thaddeus knows that.'

'The foxes aren't going to *be* anywhere near the coopssssssss,' Cleopatra said. She gave a triumphant hiss. 'My *children* will oversssssssssee the operation.'

Amy gawped at the mirror. 'I don't understand.'

'Every one of my eggs – thirty-ssssssssix in total – has been smuggled out of here today by the rats on chicken-feed lorries and placed in the nesssssssssts of broody hens,' Cleopatra explained. 'In approximately 60 days they will hatch. When they do, my babies will take control of the farmsssssss. They will force the

chickens to lay more eggs, which the rats will collect. The eggs will be taken to abandoned premisesssssss nearby and hatched out so that we can sssssset up new battery farms. Very ssssssssoon we shall have battery farms all over the country to feed the local foxssssss population. And there is nothing you and your friends can do to stop usssssss.' Cleopatra's tongue flicked in and out. 'Now enough talking. It'sssssss dinner time.'

Amy grabbed the Venombrella from the Emergency Chicken Pack. She pressed the button and lifted it over her head. *Just in time!* A shower of cobra spit splashed onto the Venombrella.

Cleopatra hissed in fury. She spat again. Amy scooped up the Emergency Chicken Pack and threw it on her back. She darted backwards and forwards with the Venombrella in her wing, trying desperately to find the snake-charming flute or the net or the rocket booster, but she couldn't see them anywhere. Cleopatra must have hidden them under the straw.

'Amy!' the cry came from the cellar steps.

Amy glanced round. She saw Ruth. And Boo. They had come back for her!

Both chickens were wearing sunglasses to protect them against Cleopatra's hypnotic stare. Ruth was carrying her self-packing suitcase; Boo held the mite blaster in her wings.

Cleopatra had seen them too. 'Choicessssssss, choicesssssss,' she chuckled, turning her head towards the steps. 'I'll start with the plump, juicy-looking one.'

Amy saw Cleopatra's coils unravel. The snake had changed direction. She wasn't chasing her any more. She was after Boo!

'No!' Amy ran after Cleopatra.

'Get out of the way, Amy!' Boo stood her ground with the mite blaster. 'This is personal.'

'But Professor Rooster said that mites wouldn't work on Cleopatra,' Amy argued.

'We're not using mites,' Ruth said. 'We're using tacks. We got them at Aunt Mildred's when we dropped the chickens off. Now duck!'

Amy crouched under the Venombrella.

Boo raised the weapon and fired.

BANG!

A cloud of tacks flew towards Cleopatra.

TICKER-TACKER-TICKER-TACKER-TICKER-TACKER.

The tacks bounced off the Venombrella like hailstones.

Cleopatra let out a terrible hiss. A few of the tacks had stuck in the queen cobra's skin. Lots more lay on the floor in a spiky carpet. Every time Cleopatra slithered forward more tacks impaled her.

'SSSSSSSSSSSSSSSSSSSS.' Cleopatra writhed and twisted.

'Ruth, open the suitcase!' Boo said.

Amy just had time to see the powerful magnet emerge from inside the suitcase, then she felt herself being lifted into the air. She landed with a bump in the suitcase next to the mite blaster, surrounded by sharp pins. 'Ow,' she said.

'Oops,' said Ruth. 'That wasn't meant to happen. It was supposed to pack Cleopatra, not you!'

Amy looked bewildered.

'Remember you told James Pond that the suitcase might defeat Cleopatra if she swallowed something metal? Well, Boo and I couldn't see how to get her to do that, but we thought the tacks might work instead. Aunt Mildred had some in her collection. That's where we got the sunglasses too.'

'Why didn't it work then? How come the suitcase packed me instead?' asked Amy.

'Because the magnet was more attracted to the mite blaster and your umbrella than it was to the tacks,' Ruth explained. 'We didn't get enough of them to stick to Cleopatra.' She helped Amy out of the suitcase.

Cleopatra was still inching her way towards them painfully. 'I can shed my sssssssskin,' she threatened, 'it doesn't make any difference to me. But once you lose yourssssssss, you're finished.'

'So, er, what do we do now?' Amy asked.

Ruth yanked the mite blaster and the Venombrella off the magnet and closed the suitcase lid. 'We'll have to try again. Boo, take the mite blaster.'

There was no response.

'Boo?' Ruth repeated. 'Wait, what's wrong with her?'

Boo was swaying from side to side, her eyes on Cleopatra. *She was being hypnotised.*

'Don't look at her, Boo!' Amy cried.

'I can't help it.' Boo said dreamily.

'The sunglasses aren't strong enough to stop the hypnosis,' said Ruth in a panic.

Cleopatra had reached the bottom of the cellar steps. She raised her head until it was parallel with the three chickens. Amy watched in horror as she

unhinged her jaws and lunged at Boo.

'No!' Amy wasn't going to let her friend die. On impulse she grabbed the Venombrella, pushed Boo out of the way and thrust herself inside Cleopatra's wide-open mouth.

Chapter Seventeen

Cleopatra's jaws closed around her. Amy felt herself being pulled forward into the snake's body by a series of powerful contractions. It was like being dragged under water by a strong wave. She tried to resist by spreading her wings and digging her heels in, but the insides of the snake were smooth and slippery. Amy knew it wouldn't be long before she reached the queen cobra's stomach. And when that happened Cleopatra's digestive juices would gradually turn her into mush.

She tried to think. There had to be a way of getting out of there.

It was then that Amy's little chicken brain had one of its rare flashes of chicken inspiration. *Burt's Burp Powder!*

She fumbled with the backpack. It was hard taking it off her shoulders – she was being squeezed on every side – but eventually she managed it. She'd have to

hurry. She could hear gurgling. It couldn't be far now to Cleopatra's stomach. Her wings trembling, Amy extracted the packet of Burt's Burp Powder. *What had the label said about the dose?* She wished she could remember. It was inky black inside the snake and she couldn't see to read it. She tried visualising the writing in her head.

For a MEGA-BELCH take one dose of Burt's Burp Powder
For a SUPER MEGA-BELCH take two doses of Burt's Burp Powder
To produce a TOXIC VOLCANIC ERUPTION the whole packet may be consumed
Note: Risk of vomiting if taken after food

That was it! Amy blinked. What she needed was a TOXIC VOLCANIC ERUPTION. She had to give Cleopatra enough burp powder to make her sick.

She opened the packet and shook all the burp powder out in the direction she was travelling – towards Cleopatra's stomach. The contractions stopped. Nothing happened for a moment. Then the contractions started again. Only they weren't taking

Amy further inside the snake any more: they were squeezing her in the opposite direction, back towards Cleopatra's mouth.

The contractions became faster and stronger. Amy tumbled forwards, clutching the Venombrella. She heard a noise like gushing pipes. *The sick was coming*! She held on tight to the Emergency Chicken Pack with one wing and pushed frantically at the button on the Venombrella with the other.

'BBLEAARCCCCCHHHHURRRRRRPPP!'

Amy lost her grip on the Venombrella. She was being regurgitated! She catapulted out of the snake's mouth back on to the cellar steps on a tidal wave of gooey cobra sick.

'Yuk!' she said, smearing gunk away from her beak. She sat up, dazed. Boo and Ruth were beside her.

Boo dabbed at her sticky feathers with some straw. 'Amy! Thank goodness! Are you all right?'

'I think so.' Amy shook goo off her feathers. Cleopatra was still retching as if she were trying to get rid of something else. Amy wondered what it could be. Then it dawned on her. *The Venombrella!*

It must have got stuck inside Cleopatra when Amy tried to open it.

'Quick, Ruth, open the suitcase,' Amy cried. 'The Venombrella's still in there. Cleopatra *did* swallow something metal after all. We can trap her with the magnet.'

'Good thinking!' Ruth wrenched open the self-packing suitcase. The magnet emerged. Its prongs turned in the direction of Cleopatra.

The three chickens threw themselves to one side as Cleopatra's body was drawn towards it. The snake thrashed her head from side to side, trying to fight the strong magnetic force. 'No!' she choked. But the magnet was too strong for her. It kept on tugging at the metal in her throat.

'You sure she'll fit?' asked Amy. The suitcase looked quite small compared to Cleopatra.

'It's expandable,' Ruth said. 'You can fit anything in there. Even a queen cobra.'

'Wow!' Amy said. 'You are clever, Ruth.'

PING!

The top of Cleopatra's long body shot towards the

suitcase, followed by her twists of brown coils. The suitcase packed her neatly inside.

'Watch out!' Amy yelled.

'BBLEAARCCCCCHHHHURRRRRRPPP!'

Cleopatra had finally managed to burp out the Venombrella. But it was too late for the queen cobra. 'I'll get you for thisssssssssss,' she screamed.

BANG! Ruth brought down the suitcase lid and locked it.

Amy lay on her back with her feet in the air. 'That was scary,' she said.

'Very.' Boo sat down next to her. 'You were really brave,' she whispered. 'Thank you for saving me.'

'That's okay,' said Amy. Then she added, 'I always knew I could get out with the Burp Powder. It was nothing really.' Of course it was a fib, but only a little one, and she thought it might make Boo feel better.

The two chickens held wings.

'Can someone please help me fix this rocket blaster to the suitcase?' Ruth said. She was struggling with what looked like a very large firework.

Amy jumped up. The mission wasn't over yet.

They still had to get Cleopatra back to the City Zoo. And retrieve her eggs before they hatched. 'Where did you find it?' she asked.

'It was under the straw with the snake-charming flute and the net,' Ruth explained.

Carefully the three chickens attached the rocket blaster to the suitcase. Most of Cleopatra was inside it, but part of her tail didn't fit. It flopped about, twitching angrily. Amy and Boo made some air holes with a tack so that she didn't suffocate.

'She's ready to go,' Boo said.

Ruth typed in the coordinates of the zoo on the rocket blaster and pressed BLAST OFF. The three chickens watched in silence as the suitcase flew out of the cellar door towards the warehouse exit.

'Good riddance,' Amy muttered. She never wanted to see a snake again ever, ever, ever, EVER, in her whole entire chicken life.

'What happened to him?' Boo asked. She pointed at James Pond.

The duck agent had regained consciousness. He was sitting up groggily. He didn't seem to be hypnotised

any more. Amy felt a bit better about knocking him out. The blow to the head had brought him out of his trance. 'Never mind about him, we've got to find Cleopatra's eggs,' she said.

'Her *eggs*?!' Boo echoed. 'You mean she's already laid them?'

Amy nodded.

'Where are they then?' Ruth said, looking around.

'That's the problem.' Amy told her friends about Virginia Fox Diamond's evil plan to create more battery farms.

Ruth whistled. 'So that was what the foxes were whispering about earlier!'

'How on earth are we going to find thirty-six snake eggs?' Boo asked. 'The rats could have hidden them anywhere. There must be loads of broody hens at the farms. And we don't even know which farms they've taken them to.'

'There must be a map somewhere,' Ruth said in her super-brainy detective voice. 'Look, there. On the flipchart.'

The chickens hurried over.

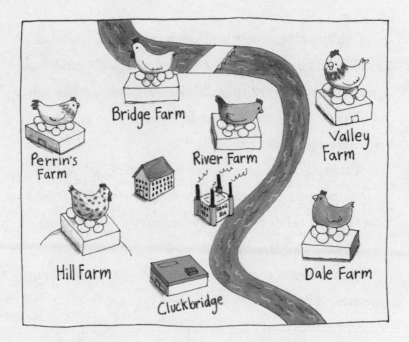

Amy looked at the map with horror. *Thaddeus had targeted Perrin's Farm.*

'Mum!' she whispered.

The others looked at her questioningly.

'Mum's broody,' Amy said in a tiny voice. 'She's sitting on a clutch of eggs. The rats might have put some of Cleopatra's babies in her nest.'

'Oh Amy, this is my fault.' Boo said. 'It was me who told Thaddeus where you lived.'

'We'll go there now and warn your mum and dad,' Ruth said firmly. 'Don't worry, Amy. We'll find the snake eggs and post them back to the zoo. Although we might need to figure out what to put them in.' She scratched her chin.

'Professor Rooster gave us a stack of boxes,' Amy told her eagerly. 'They've got stamps on and everything. They're in the Emergency Chicken Pack.'

'Good,' said Ruth.

'What about the other farms?' Boo asked. 'What are we going to do about those?'

They both looked at Ruth.

'I've got an idea about that too,' Ruth said, polishing her spectacles. 'I reckon it's time we got those beastly rats to work for us chickens for a change. *They* put Cleopatra's eggs all over the place, *they* can jolly well go and fetch them back.'

'But how can we make them do that?' Amy asked, bewildered.

'With the Stuff-a-Snake, of course!' Ruth grinned. 'We'll hypnotise the little brutes into doing what we tell them, just like Cleopatra and Thaddeus did – only

in reverse! We'll get them to go back to the farms on the chicken-feed lorries and send the snake eggs back to the zoo. That just leaves Perrin's Farm for us,' She grinned. 'Come on, you two. Let's go and wake the little beasts up.

Chapter Eighteen

On the other side of the river, Thaddeus E. Fox was finding it hard to sleep. There was very little room in the dustbin where Snooty Bush lived for one fox, let alone two, and Snooty Bush's hind legs were digging him in the ribs. Still, it wouldn't be long before they were both rich. Then he could move to a luxury garden shed of his own, and keep the old burrow in the Deep Dark Woods for weekends.

Snooty Bush shifted in his sleep. Now he had his tail up Thaddeus's snout! Grumbling to himself, Thaddeus got to his feet and climbed out of the dustbin. It was nearly dawn. He decided to take a stroll across the bridge.

He was about half way across when he heard a loud, whooshing noise above him. Thaddeus peered into the sky. His jaw dropped. A suitcase attached to a small rocket was flying over the river from the direction of the abandoned warehouse. It was heading

towards the City Zoo. Dangling out of one side of the suitcase was the tail end of a long, brown snake.

Cleopatra?!!!!!!!!??????!!!!!! Thaddeus could hardly believe his eyes. *She had been captured!* But how? It was impossible! The chickens at the battery farm were far too stupid and cowardly to stage an attack on the queen cobra, except for the plump, juicy one that belonged to Professor Rooster's elite chicken squad, and she was on death row. There was no way she could escape. An alarm bell clanged loudly in his brain.

Unless the others had come to rescue her . . .

Thaddeus let out a roar of rage. He should have eaten the wretched fowl when he had the chance. He set off towards the battery farm.

Virginia Fox Diamond was already waiting for him. 'You're too late,' she said. 'The chickens have gone. Someone opened all the cages. I think they escaped down the sewers.'

'What about the rats?' Thaddeus fumed. 'Why didn't they stop them?'

'There's no sign of the rats either,' Virginia said. 'But I found this.' She held up the limp Stuff-a-Snake. The air had gone out of it but you could still see that it was an exact replica of Cleopatra. 'I think whoever rescued the chickens has hypnotised the rats using this. My guess is they've sent the rats to collect Cleopatra's eggs from the farms and take them back to the zoo.'

Thaddeus realised he had been completely out-foxed. He let out a roar of rage.

'Those bleeping chickens have had it!' Thaddeus didn't remember ever being this angry before. He felt his lip curl and steam shoot from his ears. He thought he might be turning into a were-fox.

162

'Which bleeping chickens?' Virginia demanded.

'Professor Rooster's elite chicken squad,' Thaddeus said between gritted teeth.

'Explain,' Virginia Fox Diamond sat back and folded her paws across her chest.

Thaddeus filled her in.

It was Virginia's turn to be furious. 'You should have told me before,' she shouted. 'Why didn't you give that chicken on death row to Cleopatra straight away, or eat it yourself, you moron? Now the whole operation is in jeopardy, thanks to you.'

'Keep your fur on!' Thaddeus growled. It was easy to be wise after the event. He felt his admiration for Virginia Fox Diamond slip a little. It wasn't *his* fault the rats had been hypnotised into returning Cleopatra's eggs to the zoo. How was he supposed to know Professor Rooster would have given his chickens a Stuff-a-Snake? Virginia was being a dreadful nag.

'Well, what are you going to do about it?' Virginia snapped.

'I'm going to teach them a lesson,' Thaddeus snapped back.

'How? You don't know where they've gone.'

'Give me a minute, will you?' Thaddeus closed his eyes. *Know your enemy.* That was the number one rule of warfare. That way you could anticipate their next move and outsmart them. *What would he do,* he wondered, *if he were Amy, Boo and Ruth? Go back to Chicken HQ to celebrate? Go on holiday? Go home and relax?* Gradually his snarl turned into a smile. 'Oh, but I do know where they've gone, Virginia,' he said, his good humour returning. 'I know exactly.'

'Where?' the vixen asked.

'Perrin's Farm.'

Amy landed in the farmyard close to her parents' coop. Boo and Ruth landed behind her. They had sent James Pond back to Poultry Patrol where he wouldn't get in the way.

'Cock-a-doodle-doo!' Amy's father was just finishing his morning chorus.

'Amy!' her father came rushing towards her. 'You're back! How was the training?'

'We weren't training, Dad, I had to go on a mission,' Amy admitted. 'These are my friends, Boo and Ruth.'

'Hello,' said Ruth.

'Pleased to meet you,' said Boo.

'Where's Mum?' Amy said.

'In the coop,' her father replied. 'Most of the chicks have hatched, but the farmer gave her six more eggs to sit on yesterday, so she's still stuck on the nest.'

'The farmer didn't give them to her, Dad,' Amy said, pushing past him into the coop. 'The rats put them there when she wasn't looking.' She disappeared inside.

'The rats? What on earth is she talking about?' he asked the others in bewilderment.

'They're snake eggs, Mr Cluckbucket,' Ruth explained. 'The rats were hypnotised by Cleopatra, the queen cobra, and sent from Cluckbridge to distribute her eggs to local farms. Cleopatra was in cahoots with the foxes too. The plan was for the farm

chickens to incubate the baby snakes. Then, when they hatched the snakes would force the chickens to produce more eggs and set up their own battery farms with the local foxes nearby.'

Amy's dad whistled.

'It's our job to stop Cleopatra and send her and her eggs back to the City Zoo,' Ruth said.

'My goodness! I had no idea Amy was involved in anything so dangerous. I mean she told me about her other adventures, but this . . .'

'I expect she didn't want to worry you, especially as Mrs Cluckbucket is broody,' Boo chipped in. 'You should be very proud of Amy,' she added. 'She saved my life.'

'She did?'

Boo nodded. 'Cleopatra tried to eat me but Amy made Cleopatra eat *her* instead.'

Mr Cluckbucket gasped. 'Amy was eaten by a queen cobra? How on earth did she escape?'

'With Burt's Burp Powder,' Boo said. 'She's very resourceful.'

'She certainly is,' Mr Cluckbucket agreed.

'If you'll excuse us for a minute, we've got six cobra eggs to return to the City Zoo,' Ruth said politely. She took out the stamped-addressed boxes from the Emergency Chicken Pack.

'Be my guest,' Amy's dad stood to one side.

The two chickens bustled into the coop to join Amy.

'I wondered why those eggs were such a funny shape,' Amy's mother was saying, 'and such a peculiar colour. I thought maybe you might have laid them, Amy, they were that strange-looking!' She chuckled.

Amy didn't really mind being the butt of the joke. She was just glad they had found the eggs. 'Mum, this is Boo and Ruth.'

Amy's mum gave them a wave. 'I must say it's a relief to get off this nest,' she said, getting up and stretching her legs. 'I'll put the kettle on. We'll have some seedcake and you can meet Amy's brothers and sisters.'

'There might not be time for that,' said Amy's dad. 'Amy and her friends will need to go and collect the snake eggs from the other farms before they hatch.'

'No, it's okay actually, Dad,' Amy said.

'How come?'

'Ruth re-hypnotised the rats to make them do it.'

'That's ingenious!' Amy's dad laughed in delight. 'How on earth did you manage that?'

'With something called a Stuff-a-Snake,' Amy said. 'We'll tell you all about it once we've got rid of these.'

Amy, Boo and Ruth carefully collected the snake eggs from the nest and put them in the boxes.

'What did your mum mean when she said she thought *you'd* laid them, Amy?' Boo asked.

'I tried laying an egg when I was here a few days ago,' Amy explained. 'Only it didn't really work. I'd eaten too much popcorn and drunk too much worm juice so the egg was all knobbly on the outside and smelly on the inside. According to Mum, you have to have a balanced diet to lay a good egg.'

'Interesting,' said Ruth.

Amy chortled. 'But me and my friends had loads of fun thinking of all the silly eggs we could lay and throw at the geese!' she recalled.

'Cool,' said Boo. 'I can't wait to meet your friends.'

'Let's post these first,' Amy suggested, bringing down the lid on the last of the six boxes. 'Then I'll introduce you.'

'Okay.'

'We'll be back in a minute!' Amy called to her mum and dad.

'Where's the post box?' Ruth asked.

'At the end of the farm track. It's not very far,' said Amy.

'Won't the farmer see us?' asked Boo.

Amy checked the yard. 'No. She's out with the tractor. It's all clear.'

The three chickens put the snake egg boxes in their backpacks and strapped on their flight-booster engines.

The post box was on the corner of the road, beside the gate to the farm. The next collection was at one o'clock. Boo and Ruth handed their boxes to Amy.

'Four, five, six!' Amy pushed the last of the eggs inside the box. 'Phew!' she said, wiping her forehead with her wing. 'Thank goodness that's over.'

'Er, it's not quite,' said Ruth, adjusting her super-spec headsets. 'Take a look over there.'

Amy pulled down her headset. She blinked. About half a kilometre away, trotting along the ditch beside the road towards them were Thaddeus E. Fox and Virginia Fox Diamond. 'Barn it!' she swore softly. Now they were in trouble. If the farmer wasn't there to protect the coops, the foxes would run amok. 'What have we got in the way of weapons?' she asked.

'Nothing,' Ruth said.

'Nothing!' Amy squawked. 'What about the mite blaster?'

'We left the mite tube at Aunt Mildred's,' Boo said. 'And we're out of tacks. We used them all up on Cleopatra.'

'Bloomin' peck!' Amy exclaimed. She didn't usually swear this much, but this was turning into an emergency!

'We've still got the snake-charming flute and the net but I don't think Thaddeus will fall for that,' Boo said.

'Is there anything at the farm we can use? Anything at all?' Ruth asked.

Amy wracked her little chicken brain. It was then that she had a second flash of chicken genius.

'Maybe,' she said, her eyes gleaming. 'Come on. It's time you met my friends.'

Chapter Nineteen

Thaddeus E. Fox strolled confidently up the farm track. NOTHING COULD STOP HIM NOW. The farmer was out. He and Virginia had spotted the tractor ploughing the field a little way back. He would kill all the chickens at Perrin's Farm – every single one of them – take his pick of the plumpest and juiciest to eat and leave the farmer to clear up the remains. He didn't care any more about Snooty Bush and his battery farm. He didn't care about Virginia Fox Diamond and her chain of Foxy's Fast-Food Restaurants. All he wanted was REVENGE.

The two foxes reached the farmyard. Thaddeus took in his surroundings. The barn stood on one side of the yard, the chicken coops on the other. Behind the coops was a grassy field where horses grazed and beyond that was an orchard. A chicken pen had been set up in the orchard, but no chickens were in it. In fact, there was no sign of any birdlife anywhere.

'I don't like it,' Virginia Fox Diamond said uneasily. 'It's too quiet.'

'That's because you're a city fox,' Thaddeus said. 'In the country it's different.'

'Where are the chickens then?'

'In the coops. They're only allowed to graze in the orchard when the farmer's here to protect them. And they won't come out unless they think there's food to be had.'

'You'd better be right,' Virginia said.

Thaddeus ignored her. Virginia was turning out to be a complete pain in the brush.

The farmyard was protected by a picket fence that ran all the way around the edge. The fence was trimmed with green wire netting. They couldn't go over the top. *But they could go underneath.* Thaddeus trotted over to the gate. The ground beneath had been worn into a hollow by the farmer's boots. It was just big enough for a fox to squeeze under.

'Follow me,' he said.

The two foxes wriggled under the gate.

Thaddeus padded towards the chicken coops.

 173

'I still don't like it.' Virginia prowled anxiously backwards and forwards by the gate. 'It feels like a trap.'

Thaddeus ignored her. A string of drool hung from his mouth. He could smell chicken. They were here! It was simply a matter of choosing which coop to start on.

Just then the door of one of the coops opened. Thaddeus swung round.

SPLAT! Something soggy hit him in the eye. Egg yolk dripped down his whiskers onto his waistcoat. He wiped it off with a paw and licked it. If the chickens thought they could stop him by throwing a few soggy eggs at him they were very much mistaken.

Another door opened. Thaddeus just had time to glimpse a young chicken take aim at him with another missile before it banged shut again. He dodged.

SPLAT! The second soggy egg landed harmlessly at his feet.

'Is that all you've got?' he guffawed.

'Nope,' a voice said. A third door opened. And a fourth. And a fifth. All of a sudden doors were opening

and closing everywhere. Thaddeus felt confused. He didn't know where to look. Soggy eggs rained down on him. *SPLAT! SPLAT! SPLAT! SPLAT! SPLAT!* Very soon his fur and waistcoat were covered in sticky egg yolk. It was up his nose. It was in his whiskers. It was in his fur. He felt like he'd been bathed in glue.

'Prepare nettle egg bombs,' shouted a second voice.

Nettle egg bombs?! What on earth were they?

'Fire!'

Thaddeus found himself facing a second wave of missiles.

'Ow!' he yelped as the first one hit. 'Ow! Ow! Ow! Ow! Ow!' He twitched and jumped as the nettle egg bombs hit him. The pain couldn't have been worse if he'd lain down in a bed of stinging nettles and rolled around in it for an hour.

There was a brief pause.

'You had enough?' another voice yelled.

'No!' Thaddeus yelped. 'It barely hurts, so there.' He dragged himself towards the nearest coop.

'Okay then, you asked for it. Commence operation brick-egg bomb!'

175

From out of the orchard flew three chickens wearing flight-booster engines. Beneath them trailed three backpacks.

THUMP! THUMP! THUMP! THUMP! THUMP! THUMP! THUMP!

The brick egg bombs rained down. One hit Thaddeus on the snout, making him go cross-eyed.

Another hit him on the tail, giving him a nasty bruise. Several more hit him on the head, making him see stars.

THUMP! THUMP! THUMP! THUMP! THUMP! THUMP! THUMP!

The brick egg bombs pelted down thick and fast.

'We're under attack!' Virginia Fox Diamond shouted. 'I'm out of here!' She wriggled back under the gate and disappeared at a smart pace in the direction of Cluckbridge.

'Coward!' Thaddeus shouted after her. 'I never fancied you anyway!'

The three airborne chickens landed in the yard.

'You!' Thaddeus snarled. It was Professor Rooster's elite chicken squad.

'Do you give up yet?' Amy asked.

'I'll never give up!' Thaddeus snarled. 'Never, ever, ever, ever!'

'Okay,' Amy said, 'if you're sure.'

'Ant egg bombs to the ready!' Ruth commanded.

'Follow it up with the flies!' ordered Boo.

The three chickens took off again.

WHACK! WHACK! WHACK! WHACK! WHACK! WHACK!

Thaddeus ducked and dodged. Eggs were exploding all around him. And they were full of horrible creepy crawlies. 'Nooooo!' he screamed. Hundreds of flies buzzed in his ears. Thousands of ants crawled into his fur. They were after the sticky yolk from the soggy eggs. Thaddeus felt like a bear that had been bathed in honey and was being pursued by bees. He had to find some water to immerse himself in. He had to!

'I need water!' he shrieked.

'The river's that way,' Amy said, pointing him across the orchard.

'And don't think about coming back,' Ruth threatened, 'unless you want us to do it all again.'

'Aarrrrrrrrrrggggggghhhhhhhhhhhhhhhhhhhhhh.' Thaddeus raced off.

The chickens waited until his cries faded into the distance.

'Okay everyone, you can come out now!' Amy said.

The doors to the chicken coops opened. The chickens flocked out, rejoicing.

'That was so cool!' Amy's friends punched the air.

Amy hugged them. 'You were amazing.' She glanced at Boo and Ruth. 'We'd better fill the professor in. He'll be wondering what's going on.'

The chickens crowded into the barn. Amy's dad had rigged up an old laptop so that they could watch repeats on the Bird Broadcasting Corporation. But this time when the screen fizzled into life it was Professor Rooster who came on the monitor. 'I just heard from Poultry Patrol about the battery farm plot,' he said. 'Is everything under control?'

'Yes, Professor,' Amy reassured him. 'Everything's fine. Cleopatra and all her eggs are on their way back to the City Zoo. And I don't think we'll be seeing any more of those foxes for a while thanks to my friends here.'

Everyone cheered.

Professor Rooster smiled. His elite chicken squad had pulled it off after all. He would try to have more faith in them next time. 'Well done, everyone,' he said.

'Chicken mission accomplished. Maybe you do deserve a holiday after all.'

Epilogue

Three days later at Cluckbridge City Zoo the head zookeeper was in his office reading the newspaper.

THE CLUCKBRIDGE ECHO 30p

CLEOPATRA MYSTERY DEEPENS QUEEN COBRA'S EGGS RETURNED BY POST!

CITY ZOO

Following Cleopatra's surprise return to the City Zoo in a rocket-propelled suitcase two days ago, police have confirmed that thirty-six eggs have since been returned. The eggs were contained in individual padded egg boxes and sent to the City Zoo by post. Police

are appealing for witnesses to help trace the persons responsible but so far no one has come forward.

There was a knock at the door.

The head zookeeper put down the newspaper. 'Come in,' he said.

A woman entered dressed in a keeper's uniform. She was carrying a cardboard box.

'Ah, Cynthia, it's you.' Cynthia was the name of Cleopatra's keeper. 'Sit down.'

'Thanks, sir.' Cynthia took a seat.

'How's Cleopatra?' asked the head zookeeper.

'Moody,' said Cynthia. 'She had another pop at me this morning. Sunk her fangs right into my glove.'

The head zookeeper shivered. He didn't know how Cynthia could be so cheerful about it. 'What were you doing putting your hand anywhere near her anyway? I'll have Health and Safety on to me next,' he said.

'Because she shed her skin last night and I thought I'd better show it to you,' Cynthia replied.

 182

She opened the box, withdrew the skin and laid it on the desk.

'It's full of tacks,' the head zookeeper observed.

'I know and that's not all,' Cynthia said. 'She regurgitated these. We found them in the suitcase.' She took out a very small umbrella and a soggy cardboard carton.

'Goodness!' said the head zookeeper. 'Burt's Burp Powder! What was she eating that for?'

Cynthia giggled. 'Maybe she didn't read the label.'

The head zoo-keeper regarded her sternly.

'Stop it, Cynthia. There's no need to be facetious. Was there anything else?'

'The suitcase had wing marks on it,' Cynthia said. 'And it also contained a large magnet and some brown and grey chicken feathers.'

'What does that tell us?'

'I have absolutely no idea. Unless Cleopatra was tricked by some very clever chickens.' Cynthia giggled again.

'Don't be ridiculous,' the head zookeeper snapped. 'This is no laughing matter.'

 183

'Sorry, sir.'

'What about Cleopatra's eggs? Do you know how many she was supposed to lay?'

'Thirty-six,' Cynthia said. 'We X-rayed her before she escaped.'

'So they're all accounted for.' The head zookeeper let out a sigh of relief.

'No, sir,' Cynthia corrected him. 'We're one short.'

'What do you mean we're one short?' the head zookeeper exploded. 'It says in the paper thirty-six eggs have been returned.'

'Thirty-six eggs *have* been returned,' said Cynthia. 'But one of them isn't a cobra egg.'

'What is it then?'

'A chicken egg.'

'You mean . . . ?'

Cynthia nodded. 'I'm afraid so, sir. One of Cleopatra's eggs is still missing.'

The head zookeeper put his head in his hands. 'I'm finished!' he sobbed.

Cynthia patted his shoulder. 'Don't worry, sir, it's not as bad as you think. The egg won't hatch unless it's

incubated. So unless someone deliberately switched it for the chicken egg, everything's fine!'

'And what are the chances of that happening, do you think?' the zookeeper asked anxiously.

'About the same as a chicken tricking a queen cobra snake,' Cynthia reassured him. She packed up the bits and pieces and left the room.

Phew! Thought the head zookeeper. That's a relief! There was absolutely nothing to worry about. He picked up his paper and turned to the Sudoku.

Find out about
other crimes the
Elite Chicken Squad
have foxed . . .

Praise for *The Afterwards*

'A brave, challenging and beautifully written book that unflinchingly
confronts death, grief and denial, but which is redeemed by a dark
humour and, beneath everything, a beating heart of love'
Daily Mail

'Gravett's grey, gloom-filled illustrations, segueing into brighter
colour for the living world, combine with Harrold's restrained,
expressive text to create an extraordinary book. This is a meditative,
unsettling, tender exploration of what might happen after death'
Guardian

'Very poignant and thought-provoking ... This is a great book that
has a fantastic reach into the human world and beyond. It's a story that
will make you think and certainly reflect on life'
Mr Ripley's Enchanted Books

'Beautifully written by a wordsmith of great skill ...
Tenderness and compassion flow from every page even though this story
is not afraid to be sad and scary or even, at times, darkly funny. It's a book
about love and facing up to loss, and it's profoundly moving'
The Bookbag

Also by A.F. HARROLD

The Imaginary
Illustrated by EMILY GRAVETT

The Song From Somewhere Else
Illustrated by LEVI PINFOLD

The AFTERWARDS

A.F. HARROLD

Illustrated by
EMILY GRAVETT

BLOOMSBURY
CHILDREN'S BOOKS

NEW YORK   LONDON   OXFORD   NEW DELHI   SYDNEY

BLOOMSBURY CHILDREN'S BOOKS
Bloomsbury Publishing Plc
50 Bedford Square, London WC1B 3DP, UK

BLOOMSBURY, BLOOMSBURY CHILDREN'S BOOKS and the Diana logo
are trademarks of Bloomsbury Publishing Plc

First published in Great Britain in 2018 by Bloomsbury Publishing Plc
This paperback edition first published in Great Britain in 2019 by Bloomsbury Publishing Plc

A catalogue record for this book is available from the British Library

ISBN: HB: 978-1-4088-9431-6; TPB: 978-1-4088-9968-7; eBook: 978-1-4088-9432-3; PB: 978-1-4088-9434-7

2 4 6 8 10 9 7 5 3 1

Printed and bound in China by C&C Offset Printing Co. Ltd
Shenzhen, Guangdong

To find out more about our authors and books visit www.bloomsbury.com
and sign up for our newsletters

A tidy man, with small, hideaway handwriting,
He writes things down. He does not ask,
'Was she good?' Everyone receives this Certificate.
You do not need even to deserve it.

Douglas Dunn
from 'Arrangements'
Elegies (Faber 1985)

Hear and attend and listen; for this befell and behappened and became and was, O my Best Beloved, when the Tame animals were wild. The Dog was wild, and the Horse was wild, and the Cow was wild, and the Sheep was wild, and the Pig was wild – as wild as wild could be – and they walked in the Wet Wild Woods by their wild lones. But the wildest of all the wild animals was the Cat. He walked by himself, and all places were alike to him.

Rudyard Kipling
from 'The Cat That Walked By Himself'
Just So Stories

PROLOGUE

An old woman returns to a town she once knew.

It is a bright day. A summer's day.

From the train station she gets a taxi to an ordinary street. Stops outside a shop that was once a bakery. Gets out. Looks in the window at the absence of doughnuts.

It takes time to walk from there to the mouth of the alley. Much longer than it used to take. But then, everything takes longer now. Walking, making tea, getting out of bed.

The sound of children playing echoes in the blue sky from a field somewhere, or a playground.

She unfolds a sheet of paper from her coat pocket.

It had been forgotten for such a long time, but recently, after Mo died, and after talking to the doctor, it had risen to the top of her desk drawer. It had found its way to her hand.

She steps forward, the paper cold in the warm sunlight.

It is time, she thinks. *It's been long enough now.*
She walks by herself, into the alley.
She is looking forward to seeing the cat one more time.
She wants to say 'Thank you' at last.

December ran up the stairs two at a time, tripping at the top and knocking a pile of paperbacks over as she caught herself.

She spun on the landing, ignoring the books, and hurtled into her bedroom.

Her hair was wet and dripping and she plunged her head into a towel that had been warming on the radiator.

'Ah!' she said

Luxury.

She'd been looking forward to this for ages, thinking about it the whole journey home.

It had obviously been about to rain, but her dad had insisted they go for a walk in the woods anyway. It was what families did on a Sunday afternoon, and they *were* a family, after all.

'It's a beautiful day,' he'd said. 'I wouldn't be surprised if the bluebells are out. This is just the weekend for it.'

The bluebells *had* been out, whole rippling beds of them underneath the trees, but so had the clouds and they'd got absolutely soaked.

It had been a long walk back to the car without an umbrella.

She hadn't spoken to him on the way home.

'Shoes!' he shouted from downstairs.

The front door banged shut.

She sat on her bed and looked at her shoes.

She'd scraped the worst of the mud off before they got in the car, of course, but they still weren't exactly what you'd call clean. And they certainly weren't dry by any stretch of the imagination.

There were dark footprints leading across the carpet straight to her.

Well, it was *his* fault, she reckoned, not feeling very guilty at all. If he'd had a warm, clean towel in the car, she wouldn't have needed to hurry upstairs to dry her hair. So she wasn't to blame. Not really.

She bent down and tugged at the laces. They didn't budge.

'Knots!' she shouted.

'Ember,' her dad said from the doorway. 'There's no need to shout. I'm right here.'

He was holding the books in his hand. He set them down on the corner of the chest of drawers.

He smiled at her.

'Look at this carpet,' he said, shaking his head. 'You don't half take after your mum. Just like her.'

He knelt down and lifted one of her feet.

'Knots, you say?'

December nodded.

His fingers prised at the laces for a few seconds, and then he said,

'There you go.'

She wriggled out of the shoe and lifted the other one for him to untie too.

'What do you say?' he asked.

'What's for tea, Harry?' she replied, deadpan.

He stood up and poked her on the nose.

'Bangers and mash,' he said.

She watched as he picked his books up, the wet shoes dangling by their laces from the same hand, and went out on to the landing, pulling her door to behind him.

The 'What's for tea?' business was an old routine and they both liked it. It was easier than saying 'Thank you' and meant more or less the same thing. You just had to remember not to do it when you were stood in front of the headmaster's desk.

His name was Harry (and that was what she'd always called him, ever since she was little) and it was hard to stay mad at him for long. It was something about his smile, the width of it, the easiness of it, the quickness of it, the warmth of it. It was like a big, wobbly hot-water bottle looking at you.

December had known him ever since she was a baby – he was her dad, after all – and for as long as she could remember it had just been him and her. Her mum had gone away and they'd been

6

left on their own, her and Harry, Harry and her.

And it was all right.

That's what she thought. She knew it was all right because of that smile of his.

Her best friend from school, Happiness, had a dad *and* a mum, and they were always shouting at one another, even when December went and stayed over. She'd snuggle in her sleeping bag on Happiness's floor and listen to the noise downstairs. It was a strange way to go to sleep.

Harry never shouted at her mum. Her mum never shouted at Harry. Harry never had a bad word to say about her mum. He didn't say *much* about her, but when he did he smiled and looked at December and shook his head in a way that smelt of love.

She knew she was lucky. She felt lucky.

Having a dead mum meant even the teachers at school tried to be extra nice to her, even that time when she'd tripped up Emerald Jones in the playground accidentally-on-purpose and her tooth had come out. She got what they called the 'benefit of the doubt'.

All in all, life being December wasn't so bad.

2

'Deck! Deck!'

Happiness was shouting in the front garden.

December opened the door, feeling slightly embarrassed as usual.

Why Happiness couldn't ring the doorbell like a normal person she wasn't sure, but it had ever been thus.

They'd lived next door to one another for nearly three years and for most of that time they'd been best friends. Ness had thrown a football at a dog that had been chasing December a few weeks after she and Harry had moved in, and that was how they'd met.

Now they were in the same class at school and sat at the same table. Their hands usually went up to answer questions at the same time. Sometimes they shared answers to tests if Miss Short was looking the other way.

They swapped their packed lunches round because sometimes you needed a break from the same sandwiches and they always snapped their chocolate biscuits in two.

This Monday was the first day back after the Easter holidays and Ness had been away visiting her grandparents for the last week, so there was lots to talk about. She was excited and bouncing on her toes as they walked down the three streets that led to school.

It was all 'Then Grandpa let out this most enormous –' and 'The dog fainted, and then Gran –' and 'Mum was so embarrassed when he said –' and the like.

December dragged her heels and laughed at her friend. She could've listened to this sort of thing forever, but soon they passed through the school gates and the bell went and the register was taken and gossip had to be put to one side for a time.

In class they learnt about the Vikings. Then they climbed ropes in the gym.

They played football at lunch and December swapped her ham sandwich for Happiness's ham roll.

In the afternoon a light rain speckled the classroom windows, but it stopped by home time. There were hardly even any puddles to splash in on the way home. And so they walked together, dry-footed, skipping and swapping stories.

Yet again it hadn't been a bad day at all.

They parted on the pavement outside their houses.

'You wanna come to the park?' Happiness asked.

'Can't,' said December. 'Going out with Dad and Penny later. Gonna have to wrap a box of chocolates first, *and* have a wash.'

'Well, see ya tomorrow then.'

'Yeah, see ya.'

15

Penny was Harry's girlfriend. (Although 'girlfriend' was hardly the right word, since she was over thirty, but no one seemed to notice that.)

She was nice. Didn't try to be December's mum. Didn't try to be her bestest best friend. She was just cool. Friendly enough, nice enough, kind enough.

Tonight they were going out for a meal since it was the one-year anniversary of December walking in on them kissing in the kitchen and finding out her dad had a girlfriend. If that wasn't worth going out for a meal with starters *and* afters she didn't know what was.

That night December had a strange dream.

It was last summer and she and Harry and Happiness had gone out for the day.

This had actually happened. The dream was just a repeat, as far as she could tell.

They were driving through the safari park when all of a sudden there was a bang and the car had slumped and there was this weird scraping noise and Harry had said a word that had made December say, 'Harry, I'm shocked,' in a way that had made him laugh.

They had a flat tyre.

'Must've driven over something sharp,' he said. 'A stone or something.'

'Shall we get out and have a look?' December said, her hand already on the door handle.

'No, Deck,' said Happiness quickly. 'I don't think that'd be a great idea.'

She was pointing out the window at the lions who were lazing in the shade beneath the tree.

'Spoilsport,' said December.

'Actually,' said Harry, 'I think Happiness makes a very good point and you should listen to her wise words.'

Ness stuck her tongue out at her friend and said, 'See? Wise words!'

'So what we gonna do?'

Harry fiddled with the gear stick and tried driving forward but the noise was horrible.

'I'll ruin the wheel if I keep on,' he said.

The car behind them honked its horn. Twice. Then it pulled out and drove round them.

Harry put the hazard lights on and said, 'We just have to wait.'

'Let sleeping lions lie,' Happiness said, keeping an eye on the lions lying in the shade.

One of them was looking up, a rather scruffy-looking one with a shaggy old tatty mane, but the sunshine was bright and hot and the big cat didn't look like it was about to move.

Ember didn't like the way the cat looked at her though, as if it knew more than she did.

After ten minutes a truck from the safari park came and towed them out of the lions' enclosure and soon the car was in the car park and they were in the café and Harry was talking to the emergency repair people on the phone.

The girls played hide-and-seek among the plastic animals, tables, vending machines and visitors that filled the noisy hall, while stuffing hot dogs in their faces.

December hid behind a fat lady and moved when she moved and got almost all the way to the door before Happiness pointed at her and shouted, 'Found you!'

'You should've seen her face,' Ness laughed when they were back in the car later on. 'She thought I was pointing at her, but I wasn't, and she got all huffy and stuck her nose in the air and her chins wobbled and she waddled off, leaving you just stood there.'

'It was a good hiding place though,' December said. 'You've got to admit, yeah?'

'Better than behind a skinny bloke,' Ness laughed.

December laughed too and then she tried to explain to Harry as he opened the door and climbed into the driving seat, but the words didn't come out right and he didn't get it, but he smiled in the mirror and said, 'Very good, girls. Seat belts on. Chop, chop.'

And they drove home.

'I spy with my little eye, something beginning with "Q",' Ness said.

'Um. Koala?'

'No.'

'What about quince?'

'What's quince?'

'It's a sort of fruit, I think,' said December.

'Nope,' said Ness.

There was silence for a while and the girls both looked out of the windows at the motorway whizzing past. Green verges and green fields, sheep and trees, and the stretching blue, cloudless and endless above. The windows were open and the air was cool and fierce on their faces, and as they passed other cars they stared at the people who refused to look back at them, and they laughed.

'Qualllm?' December said eventually.

'What's qualllm?' asked Ness.

Yes, what is qualllm? thought December,

   and then she realised she was

      yawning and the car seat

         was so soft and warm and,

            almost mumbling,

               she listened to herself say,

'It's that bit when you're just falling asleep

or just waking up
and you're all peaceful and dozy and you're lying there
and you don't really remember what's real

and what's not,
but it's all quite lovely.'

'Yes,' said Ness, yawning wide, 'maybe that's it.

Falling asleep.

Waking up.
Maybe that's it.

Maybe that's what it is.'

The next morning all was silent outside the house.

Silent apart from the occasional car passing by and Mr Dibnah's dog, who had a daily walk before breakfast – a walk which neither Mr Dibnah nor the dog enjoyed.

When it was time to go to school, December went and knocked on Ness's door.

There was no reply.

This was odd.

'Maybe she's already gone,' Harry said.

'But without me?'

He just grinned and shrugged his shoulders.

'You'll be all right walking on your own, yeah?'

'Of course,' she said, pulling her bag up on to her shoulder and setting off.

'Remember to wash behind your ears,' her dad called, which

was his way of saying 'Love you' and 'Goodbye for now' all in one.

December walked quickly.

When she got to school, Ness wasn't there either.

Not in the playground, not in the classroom.

They all marched through into the hall for a special assembly.

They didn't normally have assembly on a Tuesday.

'What's going on?' December asked Toby, who was in front of her as they walked down the corridor.

'Dunno,' he said, picking his nose. 'Prob'ly a vis'ter or somefink. Maybe we're gettin' prizes or somefink.'

December looked around as they walked and wondered what sort of prizes the prizes might be.

When they were all sat down in the hall, legs crossed neatly and eyes facing forward, Mr Dedman, the head, wheeled himself out in front of the crowd.

He coughed.

He looked at them.

He looked at a sheet of paper in his lap.

He coughed again.

It was as if he didn't quite know what he was doing, which wasn't like him at all. He must've taken hundreds of assemblies in his time. You could tell because his moustache had turned grey.

Despite his name he was usually friendly and made bad jokes.

Today he made no jokes.

'Um, children,' he said, without saying 'Good morning' first. (A few little voices near the front tried echoing back the usual 'G o o d m o r n i n g, e v e r y b o d y' but they stumbled to silence halfway through.) 'Children, as some of you may have already heard, um, I've got some bad news to tell you. Last night … yesterday, after school, one of our friends, one of the brightest and liveliest girls in this school, had a … an accident. She fell off a swing in the park and hit her head. It was nobody's fault, just an accident and a very sad one. The ambulance came and took her to hospital, of course, but I'm sorry, um, to say she didn't wake up again, and in the early hours of this morning she … er, she passed away.'

There was a tremor in his voice as he spoke. A tear on one cheek. His serious grown-up face went a little wobbly as December watched. His moustache trembled and sparkled. She tried to listen to his words, but they didn't quite make sense. Who was he talking about? He hadn't said anyone's name.

She was sat next to Toby, who was still picking his nose. She didn't normally sit next to Toby.

A stone was sinking inside her.

Somewhere near the front of the hall she could hear crying.

It wasn't Mr Dedman, but some of the little kids.

'We've sent a text out to your parents,' the head went on. 'I know some of you might want to be with your families today instead of here. But I want you to know that we are your family too. The whole school is here for you, and if anyone wants to talk, please remember we are here to listen. You can talk to any of us.'

'Please, Mr Dedman,' someone said. It was a child's voice.

December looked around to see who had spoken, whose hand was in the air, and discovered it was her.

'Yes, Ember?'

'You've … you've not said her name, Mr Dedman. You've not said who it is.'

'Oh.' He looked down at his hands, coughed, looked at the wall and then at December. 'I'm sorry,' he said. 'Happiness Browne. It

was Happiness who had the accident.'

There were more tears and gasps around her. A chattering sprang up, quiet, subdued, strangled, nervous, scared, and it wasn't hushed by the teachers sitting at the edge of the hall.

The stone that had been

    sinking

       inside her

      hit

        bottom.

          Mud puffed up.

           She couldn't move.

          It was

           too

            heavy.

             'Oh,'
           she said.

She had a quiet lunch with her dad.

He'd come and picked her up from school when he'd got the message.

'Do you want to stay?' he'd asked.

She'd shook her head. School echoed with Happiness. It was too sad.

That afternoon, Penny came round to see them.

She brought cake.

She didn't know what to say.

They sat and watched television for a bit, December curled up against her dad.

The man on the screen was learning to tap dance, but wasn't very good at it.

The cake sat on the coffee table uneaten.

After a bit, Harry said, 'Not a good day, is it? I bumped into your Uncle Graham at the shops this morning. Betty got hit by a car last night.'

'Oh no,' said Penny, 'that's awful.'

Graham was December's mum's brother. He lived nearby but they didn't see each other all that often. Betty was his dog.

She was one of those dogs that's mostly shoulders and dribble. December had never much liked her.

'I'm sorry,' she said anyway.

'Oh, pet, it's not your fault,' said Penny, getting up. 'Shall I make us some more tea?'

And so the grey day went on.

It rained in the early evening, but had stopped by the time she went upstairs.

Her dad sat on the floor by her bed and read her the report he'd been writing for work until she fell asleep. She liked it when he did that.

Soon she was snoring.

December's dreams were jumbled and distant. She had the feeling
her mother had been in them, which was unusual.

She woke in the middle of the night, in the pitch dark,
and heard the rain thrumming on the windows. There was
a storm raging out there. She felt worried for the fishermen
out at sea. She liked fish. And then, in among the thudding
sting of the raindrops, she heard Happiness knocking on the
glass.

Tap. Tap. Tap.

She lay there, filled with worry.

And then, later, she woke up again and it was morning. The
light was shining through her curtains, which were never thick
enough, never heavy enough, to the keep the day at bay.

When she opened them and looked out, the pavements were
dry, not a puddle in sight.

December was quiet at breakfast.

Her dad didn't ask her what was wrong. He didn't need to.

Penny was there. She'd stayed the night, which she did every now and then.

Toast crunched slowly round the table.

Her dad walked her to school, leaving Penny to guard the house.

'You gonna be OK, kid?' he asked.

'Can't I stay home?' she said. 'I don't feel very well. I'm scared. Like butterflies.'

'I know,' he said. 'But you've gotta go. You need to go to school, and you'll be with your friends. They probably feel like you do. Don't you think?'

She kicked a dandelion that was growing out of the pavement, snapping its head off with a satisfying *snick*.

'Dunno,' she said. 'I think I just want to go back to bed. I didn't sleep well.'

'Darling,' her dad said, 'Happiness wouldn't want that, would she? She'd want you to go to school. She'd want you to be with your friends, to be with *her* friends.'

'But, Harry,' December said, 'it doesn't matter what she wants. She's not here, is she? And anyway, she liked sleeping. It was one of her most favourite hobbies.'

'Of course it matters,' her dad said, squeezing her hand. 'Of course it matters what she wants, or what she wanted. And, well … sometimes you have to guess. You have to guess, now that they're not here to tell you. You have to work it out yourself, and you do your best to do right by them.' He paused to cough a little cough. 'Ember, my love, you just try your best to do what they would have wanted.'

'You're squeezing my hand,' she said. 'You're hurting.'

He let go.

'Sorry,' he said.

She didn't ask him what all *that* was about. She thought she understood, thought she understood why it sounded as if he cared so much. He wasn't talking about Happiness any more; he was talking about her mum.

'I'm sorry too,' she said quietly.

He never talked like that normally. He usually smiled and laughed when he talked about her mum, telling December how much fun she was, how smart, how funny. He always stopped talking before it got sad, or before he got sad, although that didn't stop December from sort of missing this woman she hardly remembered, this woman she'd hardly met.

Sometimes she looked at the photo of the three of them which sat on the mantelpiece and filled that familiar grinning stranger with all the stories her dad had told her, and, yes, it was a shame she wasn't there to tuck her in at night or to wash her hair or to mend the slow puncture her bike kept getting, but it wasn't the end of the world. Her mum wasn't there in the same way a character off the telly isn't there: you might feel you know them, you might know loads about them, you might think you probably love them even, but you don't expect them to turn up to tea one day, and if they did you probably wouldn't know what to say to them anyway.

Happiness was different though. She *should* be there. Every day. And now she wasn't.

School was odd.

The day went by as days do, but quietly. Everyone was quiet. The teachers, the kids, the dinner ladies. It was a bit like being on an old ship lost at sea, becalmed and bobbing.

Eventually the final bell went and it was home time.

Her dad wasn't waiting for her at the gates, but that was quite normal. She and Ness walked home together usually. It was only a couple of streets, after all.

Today, however, she'd secretly hoped Harry would be there. She didn't fancy walking by herself.

She knew that if she'd asked him, he'd've been there, but she hadn't asked.

She pulled her bag higher up on her shoulder, and, taking a deep breath, walked out of the playground and into the road, heading for home.

'Yo, Amber,' a voice said, just as she turned the first corner. 'Where're you off to?'

Walking towards her was a man, short and stubbly, with a blonde ponytail. He was wearing a leather jacket and dark glasses and smelt faintly of dust and cigarettes.

It was her mum's brother, Uncle Graham. In ten years, he'd never once got her name right.

He rode a motorbike that took blood samples or donor hearts or other special things between hospitals, but he didn't have his bike with him this afternoon.

'Soz I'm late, mate,' he said. 'I wasn't sure what time you got out. Back in my day we were at school right up till it got dark.' He laughed, a little yapping sort of laugh that was always a surprise when she heard it come out of him.

37

'Your dad sent me. Him and Whatsername've gone off for the afternoon.'

December didn't say anything. She just listened, holding the strap of her bag tightly between her fingers and thumb. The fabric was a nice sort of rough.

'He said they'll be back about six. You can come have tea at my place. Keep me out of trouble, eh?' He laughed again.

It wasn't like her dad to go off without telling her, but she couldn't very well argue with Graham. He was her uncle and she'd been round his house before, although not very often. He only lived a few roads away from her school, but in the opposite direction to home.

Besides, she didn't have a door key, so it was either go round Uncle Graham's or sit on her front step until her dad came home.

She looked up at the clouds.

They were grey, and some of them looked grumpy.

'OK,' she said. 'But it's Ember, not Amber.'

'Course it is,' laughed her uncle, slapping her on the back. 'Course it is.'

As they walked he kept up a stream of chatter, which filled the air around them.

It reminded her of walking with Ness, except he talked less about crisps and more about TV shows she'd never seen.

December watched telly in Uncle Graham's front room while he pottered around the house doing other things. He'd made her squash and a surprisingly good tuna sandwich.

She sat on the settee with her feet tucked up underneath her. She leant her head on a cushion.

It was hard to concentrate on the programme, because her mind was elsewhere. It was as if there was something she'd forgotten to do, that she'd promised someone she'd do … something important. But she checked through and counted off on her fingers and there wasn't anything. Not really. It was just … just Happiness, she guessed.

She hadn't cried yet.

That had surprised her.

She'd've wanted people to cry for her if she died.

So maybe, she thought, that meant that Happiness *wasn't* dead.

That Mr Dedman had got it wrong in assembly and had meant to say another girl's name instead and Ness had just gone off on holiday without telling anyone.

She looked at the dog basket that was on the floor by the gas fire. The blanket was dirty and dangled half out. A rubber bone lay in the very centre of the basket, not saying anything.

'You 'K, Amber?' Graham said, poking his head round the door.

He had a mug in his hand that he was drying with a tea towel.

He gave her a smile that she recognised, not because it was his smile, but from the photo of her mum at home. They had the same smile.

'D'ya want more squash or 'nother biscuit or something?' he said. 'Give it half an hour and I'll walk you home.'

'Biscuit, please,' she said.

He went away and came back with a packet of custard creams.

'Take a couple,' he said.

Half an hour later she put her shoes on.

A phone rang.

It wasn't hers because she didn't have one, even though she'd asked her dad for one a hundred times. 'Maybe next birthday,' he'd said each time.

Graham ran past, springing up the stairs, his mobile buzzing in his hand.

'Yeah?' he said as he reached the landing. 'Oh really? … Oh no … Of course, of course … I'll let you know if I see …'

He was moving about upstairs as he talked, his voice fading in and out of earshot.

Ember went into the kitchen to pick up her school bag and when she came back into the hall, Graham was just coming down.

A dog lead made of shiny silver chain hung from a hook by the front door.

The house smelt of Betty, even though she wasn't there.

She guessed the house next door to hers would smell of Happiness, even though she didn't smell.

'Out the back,' Graham said. 'We'll go out the back. It's quicker that way.'

They went through into the kitchen and out the back door.

He locked it behind them.

The garden was just a long square of earth, with sprigs of grass and weeds poking up here and there, and with a washing line crossing it diagonally.

'I keep meaning to do something with it,' he said. 'Our mum always had it beautiful, but Betty won't be doing with flowers. She's a digger. Always digging for gold.'

He gave a chuckle and shook his head.

At the end of the garden was a gate that led them out into an alley.

Graham pulled a bit of paper from his pocket. It was scrunched up and he unfolded it sort of flat and moved it around like it was a map he was trying to find north on.

'This way,' he said, pushing past a wheelie bin.

It was odd, Ember thought, that he needed a map to get out of the alley, but she didn't say anything, not knowing what to say.

He was her mum's brother, and he *had* just made her a very decent tuna sandwich, so he deserved the 'benefit of the doubt'.

They reached a place where the alley met another one, crossing it like a T-junction.

'This way,' Graham said, turning left.

She followed.

After another twenty metres they met another alley, another T-junction.

He turned left again.

Again she followed.

Overhead, clouds drifted slowly by and she could hear a pair of pigeons cooing to one another.

Another T-junction.

Left again.

Now Ember was sure there was something odd going on. If they'd turned left and then left and then left again they should be almost back where they began. That was geometry.

'Are you sure this is the right way?' she asked.

Graham, who was a few metres ahead of her, turned and looked at her and said, 'Oh yes. This is it. It's a short cut. We're almost there. Not far now.'

Something about what he said and how he'd said it, a series of answers that tripped over each other as he'd spoken, made the hair on the back of her neck stand up.

He sounded odd. Nervous.

They went round another corner.

Should I run? she thought, and as she thought it she noticed something in the shadows.

Sat on top of a dustbin (not a wheelie bin, but one of those old-fashioned, round metal ones you see in old telly programmes) was a cat. She could hardly make it out in the gloom. It was a rough dark shape in the shadows, but she saw the flicker of its odd-coloured eyes as it slowly blinked at her. One was red; one was blue.

'C'mon,' Graham said, turning left yet again
and heading up another alley.

Not really seeing what other option
she had, Ember followed and as
she turned the corner she
looked again at the cat and
it shook its head, tattered
ears and all, as if to say,
'Don't go *that* way.'

But then it jumped
down from the bin
and padded off
in the
opposite
direction.

Graham was ahead of her,
just ten metres away
and he was opening a gate
on one side of the alley.
A gate into one of the gardens.

He looked at his piece of paper before he did so and sighed deeply.

It was an odd thing to see, that sigh, though Ember couldn't really say why.

She walked up to him.

'Are we back at *your* house?' she asked.

Turning four corners would've brought them round in a circle (well, a square), back to where they started. But she wasn't sure how many corners they'd gone round. The memory seemed muddy.

Uncle Graham didn't say anything but walked through the gate into the garden.

Looking through the gate she noticed something wrong. Something strange and wrong.

Ember had seen enough old films on the telly to know what the world looked like in black and white.

And she'd seen enough of the world to know that it was only black and white in old films.

Graham's garden (and it *was* his garden, it had the same saggy washing line across it, though the lawn looked more grassy and flowerbeds filled with flowers lined the sides) was now in black and white.

She looked at the alley around her, at the tarmac at her feet, at the wheelie bin over the way. Colour. It was all colour. Normal. Only the garden and the house beyond it were black and white. Through that gate. Not normal.

Grey and grey and grey.

'What's happened?' she said.

'Quickly,' said Graham urgently. 'Come in here, I've got

something to show you. It's important.'

She stepped through the gate.

She held her hands up in front of her face. They were still the same colour as they'd always been. So was Graham. It was just the world. (Even the sky above her was grey now, where it had been blue moments before.)

Graham unlocked the back door.

There was a noise inside. A snorting, chomping, ugly noise.

Ember took a step back, but it was just Betty, just Graham's dog, Betty, bursting out of the door in an explosion of slobber and shoulders and joy.

Graham fell to his knees and hugged her.

'Yes,' he said. 'Oh, love.'

Her tail was a crazy blur, her eyes glittered with canine adoration, her clawed feet clattered on the concrete of the back step.

She was, however, like a dog from an old film. That is to say, she was black and white, like the garden, like the house, like the world. And although she *was* a black and white dog (white with black splotches), this was something different.

They looked so happy together, Graham and Betty, as if they belonged together like a heart inside a chest. And although she'd always found the dog scary, dribbly and growly, although Betty had always looked at her from the side of her mouth like a gangster worried that someone was after her food, Ember found that the sight of the two of them together, reunited, made her smile. Warmed her.

It warmed her until she remembered.

The dog is dead.

And then she felt cold.

The dog was knocked down.

And then she felt sick.

Dead dogs wag no tails.

And then a voice spoke.

'This? You *really* want to do *this*?'

It sounded incredulous.

December spun round.

Behind her, blocking the way to the alley, was a woman.

She was tall, wide, muscly, wearing a light summer dress covered with pictures of bright flowers and skulls.

She was pointing at Ember with one hand, palm up, index finger loosely lolling in her direction.

'You would swap *this*, for *that*?'

She pointed at the dog.

Graham nodded, his hand on Betty's head, filled with love.

He didn't look at Ember.

It was almost as if he couldn't, or wouldn't.

'What's happening?' she asked, first looking at him and then at the woman. Eager to receive an answer from either one.

'Very well,' said the woman, not talking to Ember.

She stepped to one side and gestured to the back gate.

'Go. Don't look back.'

Her voice was filled with closing doors.

Graham shooed Betty out into the alley and then followed her, not looking round.

Ember thought she heard him mumble 'Sorry' as he went past, but she couldn't be sure.

Before she could move, the tall woman in the summer dress slipped through the gate into the alley too, and closed it behind her.

Ember was left in the garden. In the black and white, really weird, garden.

'Oh no you don't,' she said, getting control of herself again.

She grabbed hold of the gate handle and twisted it so the latch lifted, and pulled it open.

The alley was there, as before, except the colour wasn't and neither were the people or the dog who had, just seconds before, stepped through it.

'Oh,' she said.

December looked both ways up and down the alley.

It was grey and silent.

She stepped out and let the gate swing shut behind her.

There was no wind and her hair didn't ruffle in it.

She wondered which way she should go.

To the left, where she'd come from, was a dead end that hadn't been there before.

To the right was, instead of the corner they'd passed two minutes before, an alley-mouth that led out to a grey pavement, out to a grey street. The T-junction had disappeared.

Seeing no other choice, she heaved her school bag on to her shoulder and walked to the street.

Although it was grey and although it was silent she recognised the road. It curved round towards her school. A little way down on the other side was a newsagent's, and further along past that was a little bakery where she and Harry sometimes bought iced buns or doughnuts.

The buildings were all there and the lamp posts, but there wasn't a car to be seen, nor a person.

It was usually quite a busy road, with cars and buses going about their business, and people walking dogs or hurrying along with umbrellas or talking to a postman.

But now there was nothing. No one.

It was like Ember had woken up in a dream and everyone else had stayed asleep, as if the world had stopped and only she'd been missed out and was still moving about. She didn't like it.

It didn't make sense.

Her heart tiptoed in her chest, trying not to worry her.

Maybe if she just went home, Harry would be able to explain everything. He usually did.

So she turned in the direction of her school and started walking. Three streets past the school was home. It wouldn't take ten minutes to get there.

The two girls had been sleeping at December's house one night when they'd gone downstairs, while Harry was snoring, and drunk all the custard in the fridge. There'd been two of those big plastic tubs, which he'd bought because they'd been about to go past their sell-by date and so had been cheap.

They'd raced each other, glugging them down, and it had been a tie.

They'd crept back to bed, stifling giggles, sticky-faced and feeling swollen.

December had fallen asleep.

And she'd slept until Ness woke her up by being sick all over her sleeping bag, and then Harry had got up and dealt with everything, even though it was the middle of the night.

He might've grumbled a bit, but he hadn't been angry. He'd got the spare sleeping bag out of the airing cupboard and everyone had gone back to bed.

But when Ness's mum heard about it in the morning, she wasn't so happy. She'd shouted and pointed her finger.

'Out-of-date custard!' she'd said, shaking her head. 'Out of date! What sort of a father … ?'

Whose idea had it been to have the custard race?

December couldn't remember.

Had *she* been a bad influence on Ness or had it been the other way round?

She knew what Ness's mum would say, but she reckoned they both took the lead at different times. That was why they were such good friends. They took turns bossing each other around. Being the smart one.

But why had she thought of custard just then?

Oh!

It had been seeing the empty windows in the bakery as she went past. Normally there were trays of cakes and pastries and doughnuts, but in this grey world there'd been nothing in there. Nothing for sale. And Ness was weird. She preferred *custard* doughnuts to *jam* doughnuts.

How silly.

But maybe it was better to listen to the fluttering of a silly memory like that than the others that were lurking in the shadows and round the corners. She tried not to look at them.

And then, suddenly, as she walked she heard a noise, a clicking sound, almost a *tick-tick-tick*, and something in the corner of her eye made her turn.

There was a low brick wall keeping a front garden from spilling on to the pavement. The clicking sound came from there.

It was only a small sound, not a scary one, and December was intrigued. It was the first noise she'd heard since the world had turned black and white, since she'd been abandoned in this place.

There was a smudge in the air, a blur, on top of the wall. Not a shadow, but a brownish-charcoal smear, a hint of colour in the grey world, and it was moving. It was *something like* the shape of a bird. With every click it tapped at the concrete.

And then the bird-smudge vanished, blinked away, and something small and grey and wriggling fell to the ground.

She knelt down and saw, in the now familiar black and white, a little snail.

The tiny eyeballs rose up on the tiny eyestalks and peered around, examining her and the world, and then, after a few moments of wriggling, a wind (a wind that she didn't feel) caught hold and the snail became dust and smoke and fell apart and blew away into the air.

Gone.

'Oh,' she said,

standing up. 'Poor snail.'

She'd paid enough attention to her dad when they'd been out on Sunday walks to know that the bird-shaped smudge in the air must have been a thrush doing what thrushes do, which is cracking open snail shells to get at the snail inside. But why the bird had been a smudge and why it had simply vanished, and why the snail had been in focus and had turned to dust and blown away, she didn't know. *That* wasn't a normal part of the thrush's behaviour. Or the snail's. So far as she remembered.

She shifted the strap of her school bag on her shoulder and straightened herself up.

'OK, Ember,' she said out loud. 'Time to get moving.'

She continued on up the street, towards school and towards home, though what she'd find there in this strange empty world, this strange empty version of her world, she didn't know and wouldn't guess.

'No one's home,' said Happiness.

She'd been sitting on her doorstep, when Ember had arrived.

She looked just like the rest of the world, a girl in a black and white movie.

'I've been knocking, Deck,' she said, 'but no one answers and I don't have a key and the doors are locked and I don't understand.'

Ness was looking at Ember, but covering her eyes with her hand, as if the sun were shining in them.

Then she looked away, off to one side.

December had stopped by the wooden gate.

She didn't go into Ness's front garden but stood thinking on the pavement.

She knew she should be scared, should be afraid, but instead a big, open, confused emptiness was inside her, and her thoughts echoed.

'Ness?' she said, after a silence. 'You're supposed to be dead.'

'Oh,' said Happiness, scratching the back of her head.

Ember wondered if she shouldn't have said what she just said. What if Ness hadn't known? What if it wasn't true? What if … ?

'I thought it must be something like that,' her friend said, looking at the ground and scuffing her toe across the tiles of the path. 'That's why it's so quiet. What happened?'

'You fell off a swing.'

'Oh,' she said again. The way she said it made it sound like these surprises were only small ones, like finding 2p on the floor. Nothing to get excited about. 'That's a bit silly, isn't it? I've fallen off swings loads of times before without dying.'

'This time you hit your head,' Ember explained. 'Probably on one of the metal posts, I expect. Mr Dedman didn't say exactly.'

'Did it hurt?'

'I dunno. You're asking the wrong person. I should be asking *you* that.'

Happiness almost smiled, but it was a grey and hopeless attempt. She didn't look at Ember.

'I don't think it hurt. I don't remember it hurting. But then again I don't remember falling, so …'

She let the words trail off into dust.

December pushed the gate open and took a couple of steps up the path.

'I'm so sorry,' she said.

'What for?'

'For not going to the park with you. For not stopping you from dying. You know … that sort of thing.'

'Oh, I'm sure it wasn't your fault,' Happiness said. 'Accidents happen.'

'Yes, but …'

The emptiness in Ember's inside had become, as they'd talked, a whirlpool that she felt herself being drawn into.

Happiness was dead. And Betty, the dog, had been dead too. And she'd seen that snail die when the thrush had cracked open its home. And she was in this silent world. Where the dead … lived.

So the question spun itself around to face her: did that mean *she was dead too?*

She looked at her hands.

They were still the colour of a living person's hands.

Her school trousers were grey, but the usual, normal, *real* grey they'd always been, not the grey of a silent movie. Not the grey of Ness. And her jumper (oh!) was still red, bright like blood.

December wasn't dead.

She didn't feel dead.

Nothing had *happened* to make her die.

'What do we do now?'

'I don't know,' said Ember, and she went and sat next to her friend.

She put a hand on Ness's knee.

It wasn't cold, but it wasn't warm either.

At least it was there; at least Ness wasn't just a ghost that Ember's hand passed through.

Ness pulled her knee away. Brushed at it.

'It stings,' she said. 'Sorry.'

For the first time in their friendship December wasn't sure what to say.

They sat in silence for a bit, looking out at the street, out at the houses opposite.

Over their roofs a black circle was sinking.

It was the sun.

Shadows stretched towards them across the road.

'Hang on,' said Ember. She'd just remembered something important.

She pulled her bag up and got her lunchbox out.

Something rattled inside it.

She held the chocolate biscuit up and snapped it in two.

'Halves?' she asked.

She hadn't eaten it at lunchtime because she'd not felt hungry then.

'Thanks, Deck,' said Ness, 'but I'm not hungry.'

December *was* hungry, so she ate the whole biscuit. Both halves.

And then, as she licked the last crumbs from her fingers, something happened in front of them.

On the top of the wall that separated the front garden from the street another smudge appeared in the air. A smudge like she'd seen when that thrush had killed the snail, but bigger.

It wasn't bird-shaped this time, but cat-shaped.

In the blurred jaws the distinct shape of a struggling small bird appeared.

It was a robin, Ember could tell, and it slumped, suddenly still, in the mouth of the cat – a scruffy, battered old alley cat, the sort you wouldn't want coming through your cat flap while you were having your breakfast.

It dropped the bird, shook itself, and sat up, looking at the two girls, looking solid and as real as anything.

At its feet the black and white robin fluttered, hobbled up, fit and unbroken, hopped away, leapt into the air, and flew up to perch on a telegraph wire, from where, after a few seconds, it vanished, blown away in a streaming cloud of dust, just like the snail had been.

But the cat remained.

Ember noticed its eyes. They were different colours. One was red and one was blue.

'You shouldn't be here,' it said to her. 'Not yet. I've come to take you back.'

With everything else that had happened this afternoon she felt she shouldn't have been too surprised by a talking cat, but she was.

'Oh,' she said.

'It's a cat,' said Ness.

'Yes,' Ember said. And then she said, 'I saw you before,' to the cat.

'I saw you too,' said the cat. 'I didn't like that man. So I followed.'

'He left me here,' Ember said. 'Wherever here is. Is this heaven?'

The cat looked at her. And blinked.

'It's just a place that happens to the dead,' it said after a pause.

'Are you dead?' Ember asked.

'I'm a cat,' the cat said.

'Am I dead?' she asked.

'No,' it replied.

Happiness didn't say anything. That wasn't like her.

There was a whistling out in the street and the woman in the bright dress, its colours a startling fresh tang in the grey world, was walking towards them.

'You,' she said, 'shoo.'

She waved her hands and the cat jumped down from the wall, on the opposite side to the girls, so they never saw where it went.

'You can't stay here,' the woman said, walking up the path and looking at December. 'I've thought about it and I've made a decision. The deal is off. I'm going to give you back.'

'Back?'

'To where you belong. Not here. Back to your own people.'

'Oh,' said Ember.

'Just come with me. It won't take a second. We'll go the short way.'

She held her hand out for December to take.

'But what about …' Ember said, looking at Ness, who was still sat on the doorstep.

'It stays here,' the woman said.

'I won't go without her,' Ember said.

Happiness looked at her, blinking as if she was staring at a bright light, and then she looked down, having said nothing.

'It won't be here for long,' said the woman. 'Dust on the wind soon.'

'No,' shouted Ember. She hated hearing people talk like this, talk as if nothing could be changed, as if bad things were just things that happened, as if her friend didn't count for anything, as if she were an 'it' and not a 'she'. She hated this woman, whose dress was so colourful and whose smile was so warm, in this world of grey and shadow and silence.

She spun round and pointed at the woman, fire in her veins.

'No! I won't leave her behind. I won't leave her on her own in this horrible place. Bring her with us. Take her home. You've got to –'

'I *have* to do nothing,' the woman snapped, her voice become thunder. 'You *cannot* command me.' Then she softened.

Shook her head. Breathed. 'Don't you realise, girl, I'm doing something good for you?' She laid her hand on Ember's upper arm. Her touch was ice cold and iron strong. 'People have offered me fortunes and lives and empires to do this for them. But you get this one for free because I'm Just.'

Before Ember could say,

'Just what?'

she felt a lurch in her stomach 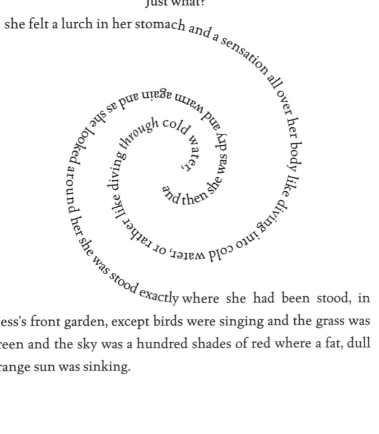 and a sensation all over her body like diving into cold water, or rather like diving through cold water and warm and dry and then she was warm again and as she looked around her she was stood exactly where she had been stood, in Ness's front garden, except birds were singing and the grass was green and the sky was a hundred shades of red where a fat, dull orange sun was sinking.

And Ness was gone.

The doorstep was empty.

'Ember? Ember!'

It was her dad's voice.

He was in the front garden next door, in their own front garden.

'Where have you been? We've been worried sick. We've phoned everyone and no one knew where you were. I've been out looking. Penny's out on her bike, trawling the streets right now.'

The woman let go of her arm, turned to face Ember's dad, and smiled.

'I spotted her wandering near the park,' she said. 'I brought her home for you.'

'Who are you?'

'Ms Todd. I work for Social Services.' She handed Harry a card that she produced from the air. 'I'm at the school for the next few days, in case any children need to talk about what happened. I'm there to listen. To support. You know.'

She smiled and leant her head to one side.

'Oh, of course.'

Harry looked at the card. Read it. Seemed to be satisfied with what it said.

Ember said nothing, looking from one grown-up to the other.

She was trying to decide if this story was better than the real one. Which would get her into more trouble?

Her heart skipped strangely inside her chest. Happiness was in her head.

'It's perfectly natural that some of the children are upset, want to seek out a little solitude, a little time of their own. This one wandered. I thought it safest I brought her home.'

'Thank you, Ms Todd,' Harry said. 'But that's the wrong house.'

Ms Todd laughed and said, 'I see that now. I guess we're all a bit absent-minded today, aren't we?'

That evening, after Ember had had a bath and once she was sat up in bed, her dad came and sat on the floor beside her.

'You know you can talk to me,' he said. 'You can talk to me about anything. Anything that's on your mind.'

She nodded.

'And you know I'm not mad, I'm not angry, but I was just so worried when you didn't come home. December, darling, don't ever do that to me again. Promise me? Penny was so worried. You know that she loves you too, don't you?'

She nodded.

Of course she knew that.

When December woke she lay in bed, making a list of new things she knew, or thought she knew.

She traced them out on the ceiling.

Firstly, the dead *sort of* don't die. There's a place where they live on for a bit. It's boring and grey and silent and she didn't want to go back there.

Secondly, her mum's brother, Uncle Graham, had made some sort of 'deal' with that Ms Todd person to get Betty back from that place. It seemed like he'd *swapped* Ember for Betty. A live girl for a dead dog.

Thirdly, Ms Todd said that she'd changed her mind about the deal. Ms Todd had brought her back from that black and white world just by touching her arm. She clearly wasn't a normal grown-up.

Fourthly, last night Harry had told her that even Uncle Graham had been out looking for her. But Uncle Graham had known full well where she was when she was missing.

Fifthly, she'd not told Harry and Penny that Uncle Graham had swapped her, in the world of the dead, for his dog. Partly because they wouldn't have believed her, but also because there'd've been all sorts of fuss. She hadn't *exactly* gone off with a stranger, but still ...

Sixthly (or fifth-and-a-halfly), she hadn't needed to get her uncle in trouble because she wanted to talk to him. She wanted him to tell her how he'd made this 'deal' with Ms Todd.

And seventhly, and every-other-numberthly, Happiness was still there, in that other place, and Ember missed her, wanted her back. The world was too quiet without her.

She went to school as usual.

Harry walked with her, but she didn't listen to what he was saying because she was making plans in her head. There were so many things she wanted to do and they all rolled around inside her like kittens in a washing machine. Every now and then she'd see a little face pressed up against the glass and it made sense, but mostly it was just a jumble.

'You promise me?' her dad said.

'What?'

'Have you been listening to a word I've been saying?'

'I was thinking.'

'Just like your mum,' he said. 'Off in your own world.'

He ruffled her hair.

They were at the school gates.

'I said,' he said, '"Make sure you come straight home after school." That's all. Or do you want me to come and pick you up? Or Penny could?'

She thought for a moment.

'I'll be fine,' she said. 'Straight home after school. I promise.'

'I love you, Ember,' he said and kissed the top of her head.

'Harry!' she said, feeling shocked and looking round to check whether anyone had seen.

She ran off through the gates and up the path to the playground.

School went ahead.

They learnt some more about Vikings.

They were making a longboat to go on the wall.

She spent the class before break making shields out of tin foil and paper and glue, to go on the side of the ship, but she was thinking about other things as she cut and shaped and stuck.

She was buzzing with secrets. There was no one she could talk to, though, no one she could tell. Her classmates would think her bonkers. Even Vincent, who'd once seen a ghost, would look at her weirdly, and her teachers would think she was just upset and confused because of … because of what had happened. Oh! She needed Happiness there. She was the only one who would've understood, who would've been as excited as Ember.

At break they were all let out on to the playground. The field was too wet still, after the recent rain, and they weren't allowed on it.

Nevertheless, when Amanda was knocked over by a football she was trying to head and everyone rushed round her on the tarmac, Ember slipped past the side of the school building and on to the field.

It wasn't very muddy at all.

Her heart was banging against her ribs, like a bird trying to escape a cat.

She'd never done anything like this before.

She ran, half tiptoeing, half skipping, across the grass, until she reached the row of trees that split the field in two.

She leant her back against the first one she came to, the school out of sight behind her, and tried to get her breath back.

Oh gosh.

Was she really doing this?

She could imagine the trouble she'd be in when everyone went in from break and they realised that she wasn't there.

She'd never done anything like this before.

Miss Short would go crazy. She'd probably phone Harry, and he'd go crazy too.

But later, when they all saw what she'd done (if she did what she hoped to do), then all the trouble in the world, and more, would be worth it.

With her heart still flapping wildly, but her breathing a little more under control, she ran across the field to where the chain-link fence was loose and slipped under it, out into the street.

From there it was only five minutes' walk, past the newsagent's and past the bakery (the window filled with doughnuts and pastries and coconut slices), past the buses and parked cars and the people out walking dogs or pushing shopping trolleys or talking to the postman (they looked at her as she went by, but she ignored them, trying to look like a girl who had been allowed out of school for a special reason, and not like a truant), to Uncle Graham's house.

She'd never done anything like this before.

His motorbike was parked on the street.

The pannier in which he carried organs from hospital to hospital glowed.

The whole world glowed. So alive.

She rang the doorbell.

Inside there was silence, and then thunking and a crash, and then footsteps, and then the door opened a crack.

'Yes?'

A sliver of Uncle Graham's face appeared in between the door and the frame.

The eye she could see was red and veiny, as if he had been up too late.

It took him a moment to recognise her.

'*You?*' he said.

He turned pale, missed a breath and stepped backwards.

The door swung open a little wider.

'No,' he said. 'You're … You can't be …'

She was sure that Harry had phoned him the evening before to say that she'd come home, but maybe Uncle Graham hadn't been listening properly, or maybe he'd somehow forgotten.

He was slowly swaying as he stood there, at the foot of the stairs, staring at her as if he had been punched a knockout blow by a huge boxer.

She pushed the door open and stepped into the hall.

A purpose was in her heart.

She wasn't afraid and she wasn't uncertain.

He stepped back.

'Tell me how to do it,' she said.

'What? Do what?'

He held on to the newel post as he spoke, but his eyes were

shuffling their feet nervously, as if really he was scared, cornered, confused. He seemed smaller than she'd ever seen him before, even though he was the same size as ever.

'Bring her back.'

His mouth hung open and he didn't say anything for a moment.

'How did you … ?' he asked eventually.

'Never you mind,' she said. 'If you don't show me how to bring Happiness back from the dead, then I'll tell Harry what you did.'

'You what?'

'You heard. I'll tell him you brought me back here after school and that you knew where I was all along … You knew where I was when they were all looking for me.'

She didn't mention the other thing he'd done, the worse thing, the thing no one would believe, but she saw it fly across his face anyway.

He stepped backwards, half staggering as if he wanted to put more space between them.

'Oh,' he said.

And suddenly he began crying.

Little sobs that caught in his throat.

He wiped his nose on his arm.

The hair glistened like a snail trail.

Seeing him like this was the first thing that wobbled Ember's resolve. She hadn't expected him to cry. She'd just expected him to help.

This man who raced round the country on his motorbike, saving lives, delivering the heart or the kidneys in the nick of time for the operation that would give someone a second chance … she hadn't expected him to break down. He was a grown-up. Grown-ups weren't supposed to cry.

He slumped down on to the stairs, and sat on the bottom step looking past her and weeping.

She went into the front room to look for a box of tissues or a hankie or something to give to him, but she didn't find a box of tissues.

She stopped in the doorway.

There, beside the gas fire, was Betty's dog basket, and in it was Betty, and she wasn't moving.

She was in colour now, like a real live dog, but she wasn't moving.

Ember tiptoed closer.

It didn't look like the dog was breathing. The ribcage wasn't going up and down or anything.

'Amber, don't …'

Her not-quite-name rippled out of the hallway between sniffs and snurfs, and lingered in the front room like a raised hand.

Looking back she could see Graham on the stairs, through the banisters. He was looking at her, looking at Betty.

She turned back.

Betty was dead. Dead again.

He'd brought her back from wherever that place was, from the black and white world, from the underworld, the afterworld, only for her to die again.

But then she thought about Ms Todd, big and bright and brutal, and of how she had said the deal was off. How she had brought Ember back when Ember should have been left there. He'd *swapped* her life for Betty's, hadn't he? That *had* been what he'd done, hadn't it?

So when she came back, the re-alived Betty must've died again. Was that how it had worked? (She saw a see-saw in her mind, one end raised up in the world of the living, one dipped down in the world of the dead. A set of scales having to balance one side with the other.)

She'd never liked Betty, but knowing that she'd snatched away the dog's new life made her feel like a cheat for a moment, made her feel like it was *she* who'd done something wrong.

She laid a hand on the dog's side.

It was cold.

It wasn't breathing.

It felt like the threadbare stuffed fox that the kids dared each other to touch whenever there was a school trip to the town museum.

But then the head swung up and looked at her with milky

white eyes and the jaw lolled open, hanging down from the head like that of a broken puppet, and a noise like a gurgling bark, a woof lost underwater and far away, crumpled out of the mouth and fell to the carpet.

December leapt back as Betty staggered to her feet, unsteady and leaning, and then slumped into her basket, grumpling and gurgling.

Drool drippled on to the tartan blanket, and then she was still again.

Ember felt sick but was pinned in place.

She didn't want to turn round, didn't want to look away from Betty, in case she moved again. But she could feel Graham's eyes watching her from behind. They tickled like cold and long-nailed fingers.

'She was fine,' he said. 'Fine when we came back. Just like ever, Amber. She was perfect again. And then … something changed.' He paused. Sums added up in his head. Gears crunched sand and dust as they rolled together. Then he spoke again. 'You,' he said. 'You've come back. She said …' But he trailed off again and never said what she'd said, or who the 'she' who'd said it had been.

Betty hadn't moved since that strange, lolling lunge, so December dared to turn her back.

Graham was on the second from bottom step of the stairs, wiping his nose on one arm, drying his cheeks with the other, and staring at her through the doorway.

He was no longer the slumped-in-sorrow ex-dog owner he'd been a minute before; now he had become something else. He had become, she saw, a man who'd found someone to blame.

What had seemed like a good idea at the time, a crazy but overwhelming idea, now felt like a mistake.

She would do *anything* to bring Ness back, of course she would, but asking Uncle Graham how he'd done it had not been the right move. Why did she ever imagine *he* would help *her*? He'd been willing to leave her *there* for the sake of an ugly old dog. Why would he suddenly help? He didn't even know her right name.

And now he was starting to get up, to heave himself up.

He was bigger than she was, and now he hated her. A black spark had sprung up in his chest. The dog he had worked some magic to save, *she* had taken from him. She didn't think he would forgive her.

A dark fire in his brain, twisting like a worm.

Her only hope was to dodge him, to outrun him.

As she thought this she was surprised to find that she was already darting past him down the hallway.

He was between her and the front door, so she was heading to the back.

Into the kitchen.

She skirted the big wooden table and slammed into the

back door, rattling the handle.

It turned easily, but the door was locked.

She looked around for a key.

It wasn't in the keyhole. It wasn't on the side. It wasn't on the table.

'Amber!'

He wasn't rushing.

He knew she was trapped.

He walked slowly along the passage.

She could feel his eyes on her.

There was a scrabbling sound too, and a thin whining, as if something else were coming towards her as well.

And then … there it was!

Hanging on a hook to one side, near the top of the back door, was the key that would let her out.

It was beyond her reach, and even when she jumped for it her fingertips only just brushed it, barely nudged it, set it wobbling.

Gasping, she tugged a chair out from under the table and climbed up on it, putting a hand on the work surface beside her to keep her balance.

She hooked the key down, but paused as she felt what her other hand was touching.

It was a sheet of paper, folded and folded again.

It was cold to the touch, in just the way paper never usually was.

'Amber, we need to talk,' Graham said as he stepped into the kitchen.

'No,' she said simply, without listening to herself.

She risked turning her back on him just long enough to get the key in the keyhole.

Her hands were shaking and it took go after go to do, but then, at last, it was in.

As she turned it, she glanced over her shoulder.

Graham was looking away from her. Looking down and behind him.

In the dark of the hallway, back there, Betty was staggering after her master, short and dribbly and whimpering.

The lock clicked and she pulled the door open.

She knocked the chair over on her way out and slammed the door behind her.

She ran through the scrubby little garden and yanked open the back gate.

Out into the alley and off to the right.

She risked pausing for a second, leant on her knees and took several deep breaths.

She was surprised to find that she still had the key in her hand. She shoved it in her pocket.

Oh! Why had she left school? Why had she run away? She

was going to be in so much trouble.

She heard the back door opening, and although she couldn't make out the words, she heard Graham shouting for her.

She ran.

Down the alley and left at the junction.

The more corners she could put between them, the happier she'd be.

Another junction and left again.

And on, and again.

And then she slowed down.

There weren't supposed to be *any* junctions in the alley. Not in the *real* alley. It ran straight out to the road.

The folded sheet of paper in her hand shivered.

She looked down at it, surprised.

She didn't remember picking it up.

It was most odd.

She unfolded it.

Before it had felt cold to the touch, and it felt colder now.

It was a map. Or, at least, sort of.

There was an odd square spiral shape in the middle and writing she couldn't read round the outside.

The ink it was written in was black. Blacker than any ink she'd seen before, which was, she realised as soon as she'd thought it, a really odd thing to think. Black was black. But still …

As she looked, the spiral seemed to revolve, to go round, but it wasn't moving.

Obviously an optical illusion, she thought. Harry had shown her them on the internet. It wasn't anything unnatural, but that knowledge didn't slow her heart down.

She couldn't hear anyone behind her in the alley. Maybe she'd lost Graham; maybe he'd been left behind somewhere where there weren't any junctions.

She must be somewhere in between, she thought as she slowly walked forward to the next junction, not quite *there* yet, but not quite *here* either.

'Somewhere you shouldn't be,' said a voice.

The cat was sat on the same dustbin she'd seen it on the day before.

'Go back,' it said.

'I can't,' she replied.

'Going on is not an option either,' the cat said. 'Not for you.'

'I need to save my friend,' she said. 'I need to go on.'

She walked past the cat. She'd come this far and she was right: she couldn't turn back. Wouldn't turn back.

Behind her the cat scratched at one of its tatty ears.

Blinked its odd-coloured eyes.

Stepped away and

v a n i s h e d .

She opened the gate and, as before, stepped into a world where all the colour had been washed away

The alley was still bright behind her; sunlight fell on the fence opposite, turning it fiery green and brown and orange.

The garden before her was grey and grey and grey.

She stepped in and shut the gate.

She waited a moment, and then opened it again.

The alley wasn't grey.

She heard a bird singing somewhere out there.

This was still the door back to her world, back to the world of the living.

Maybe it stayed open until someone went through it?

Someone living?

Someone dead?

How could she know?

Yesterday the alley had become grey and cornerless only after Graham and Betty and Ms Todd had gone through the gate. When they'd left her behind.

She needed the black and white alley though, to get out to the black and white street.

She opened the gate again, just to check, and it was still colourful.

So she wasn't going to find Happiness by going that way, not this time. She turned back to the house.

It looked just like Uncle Graham's house.

She ducked under the washing line and walked up to the back door.

It was locked.

She folded the piece of paper, the strange, cold spiral-map that had opened the alleys, and tucked it in her trouser pocket. She pulled the key from her other pocket.

It fitted and the door opened easily.

Inside was dark.

It was still.

Dust.

Her nose tickled with the desire to sneeze.

She stepped in.

She tiptoed through the kitchen, which was more or less the same as the one she'd been in just minutes earlier, except …

the table was different … smaller, in a different place. Were the cupboards arranged differently too? It was hard to tell. She'd only ever seen the room a couple of times.

She went through into the passage and down to the hall.

On her left the stairs went up into darkness.

Shadows flickered between the bannisters.

On her right the door to the front room was ajar.

She remembered Betty's basket in there, back in the real world. She remembered it being empty, and she remembered it being full …

With shaking fingers she twisted the latch on the front door and opened it.

Out there was the grey street she'd hoped for.

She looked around in the hall for something to block the door with. She couldn't let it click shut after her or she'd never get back in, and as far as she knew the only way back to life was out the back gate …

There was an umbrella stand full of walking sticks that she was sure hadn't been there in Uncle Graham's house, but which felt solid and real enough when she touched it. (So whose house was this?)

She pulled a bundle of sticks and umbrellas out and laid them in the doorway so the door could swing to but couldn't close.

She just had to hope no one came along to tidy things up.

As she pulled the door open and lifted her leg to climb over the brollies, she heard a noise.

It came from the front room, from just behind the half-open door, from that room where the dog had been.

But it hadn't sounded like a dog. Not a bark or a woof or a yelp.

It had sounded more like a chair moving, or maybe someone moving in a chair. Springs and creaking. A sigh. A breath of some sort. And now her ears were open, she realised there'd been a low buzz, a hum, a rustle in the house all along. The atmosphere crackled faintly.

Whose house was this?

When the creaking, shifting sound didn't come again, she hopped over the sticks as quietly as she could and, not daring to look over her shoulder, walked on.

And so, out into the street.

And so, out into the world.

And so.

The silence of the world smothered her. No bird sang, no car roared, no voice laughed.

Even her footsteps were dulled, softened, hushed.

Whenever she looked behind her, there was no one there. Just the black and white and empty reflection of the world she knew.

Passing the school, she looked at the playground.

She and Happiness had run around there like idiots, arms out like fighter planes, shooting each other down, before falling in a heap and laughing. So many times. So often. So simple.

That was what she remembered most. Laughter.

They sometimes laughed until they cried, not always at anything particularly funny, just *because*.

She hurried on.

Happiness was sat on the doorstep where December had left her the day before.

She covered her eyes with the back of her hand as she looked up, as if she were blocking out the sun on a summer's day.

'Deck?' she said.

Her voice was flat, quiet.

'Yes, it's me. I've come to rescue you.'

Ness lowered her hand. Looked away.

'I didn't think you'd come back. That woman ...'

Woman?

'Ms Todd?' Ember said.

'I don't know her name. The one who took you away just now.'

Just now?

'Just now?' Ember said.

Ness looked confused.

'It was just now, wasn't it?

Or was it years ago?

I don't know.

I feel so odd.

Like I'm not myself,

like I'm asleep

or falling asleep.

And then I look up and the sun hasn't moved. Nothing's happened.'

Ember looked behind her, over to the houses on the opposite side of the road where she'd seen the black sun setting the day before. And there it was, round and black like a hole in the sky, exactly where it had been before. It hadn't moved, had it?

And as she looked at the sun, she was startled by a movement. Not in the sky, but in the house below.

A curtain twitched.

A net curtain in an upstairs window moved to one side and she saw a face looking out.

The curtain fell back again and the face was gone.

'Mrs Miłosz,' Ness whispered, having seen what Ember had seen. 'She scares me. She looks at me. Watches me. And I've got nowhere to go.'

Mrs Miłosz was an old lady who had lived opposite the girls until the previous summer. She'd fallen down the stairs and the district nurse had found her. Ember remembered the ambulance. She'd never seen one in her street before. It had been exciting – the flashing lights, the colours, the sheer boldness of the thing sitting there on her street.

Mrs Miłosz's sons had come and cleared the house with a big van the following week and a new family moved in a few weeks after that and soon the whole affair had been forgotten.

Ember was silent for a moment, spiders crawling across her skin.

'The woman?' she asked. 'You were saying something about Ms Todd.'

'She said you wouldn't be back,' Ness said. 'She said I was to forget you, that I was to forget everything. She told me not to hope. "Don't hope any more," she said.'

'Well, ignore her. Forget about *her* instead,' Ember said. 'She was wrong. I found a way and I've come to take you back. To take you back home.'

She explained, as quickly as she could, trying to make it make sense in her head as she said it, about the deal Uncle Graham had made. Explained how he'd swapped her for Betty – how leaving a live person behind had let him take a dead one back. 'But,' she added quietly, 'the important thing is he found a way to here, from there. And the gate's open now, it's open back to the real world. I checked. There's still sunlight and colour out there. If we both go through it together, then we'll be in the alleys and we can go home. Nothing can go wrong.' She added that last bit, not because she believed it (she was being careful not to believe in anything too much) but to sound confident for Ness.

She put her hand out, ready to haul her friend to her feet.

'Come on,' she said.

Ness had nodded as Ember had talked, but she didn't seem excited, didn't seem to want to do anything but sit down.

'I don't know,' she said eventually, with something like a sigh.

'Maybe I should just stay here.'

Oh. It was as if when all the colour had been drained from her, all the energy had gone too, all the spark that used to be there. The Ness Ember knew would've jumped to her feet, would've shouted an enormous 'Yes!' to the sky, would've been the first one to make an adventure of it.

(Was she greyer now? Flatter than the first time they'd met here? Ember didn't want to think about it too hard. Sometimes if you asked questions you learnt the answers, and answers aren't always good things to hear.)

Being dead had changed her, and knowing that meant that Ember forgave her. She was sure, she hoped, that going back to the world of the living, getting some colour back into her, taking her back to her mum and dad would bring the old Ness back. She didn't doubt that the old Ness was just hiding, was just underneath the grey, but knowing that, and forgiving her, couldn't stop the frustration bubbling up.

'I bunked off school to bring you back from the dead,' she said, louder and sharper than she'd intended. 'I'm gonna be in *so much* trouble if I don't bring you back.'

She really didn't mean to snap, really didn't want to sound (or be) angry with her friend, but *something* needed doing.

'Come on,' she said, getting her hand round Ness's wrist and pulling her to her feet.

Ness said nothing, but stood up, shaking her wrist free and rubbing at it.

'Sorry,' she said. 'That hurt.

It stung.

Burned.'

But still she followed Ember

up

the

chequerboard

path

and

out

on

to

the

pavement.

Friends, still.

🐈

As they walked through the familiar but alien-looking streets, Ember tried to keep a stream of jolly chat going. *It's what you do when your friend's feeling down, isn't it?* she told herself. But it was hard because Ness didn't join in.

'So Harry said,' she continued, 'that I can have a phone for my next birthday and I'm worried he's gonna get me one of those pink ones with sparkles and stickers that you can use to individualise it for yourself. But I just want one that works and doesn't look stupid, but he still reckons I'm a little girl and that I want everything to be pink all the time ...' This wasn't true. Harry didn't think that and she knew it and felt bad saying it, but she had to say something.

Ness just nodded, and said, 'Oh yes?' every now and then, but she wasn't coming up with any stories of her own. She wasn't making an effort to help Ember out.

She was blunted.

'So there was this programme on telly last night,' Ember tried, 'about this bloke who collected the labels from soup cans. Not soup cans themselves, just the labels, and he got arrested in the supermarket once for peeling the label off a can he'd never seen before when he didn't have enough money to buy it, and then when the soup company heard about it they sent him a whole box of tins of soup because it had been such good publicity for them, but the thing was he hated soup, couldn't stand the stuff, so he took the labels off and gave the tins away to the local food bank. He wrote the flavours on in marker pen, because he wasn't stupid, but they wouldn't take them because of health and safety, even though there were people who could've really done with some soup. But you can't go round giving out tins of soup with the names written on in marker pen because … well, you can't really trust a bloke who goes round writing on tin cans with a marker pen, can you?'

'Suppose not,' said Ness.

They'd long passed the school and were now about to turn into the road where Uncle Graham lived.

At the corner, Ember stopped walking.

She tugged at Ness's sleeve and stopped her too. (She was careful to not touch her this time.)

'What is it?'

'Look,' said Ember.

'It's that woman,' said Ness, turning away.

There, halfway down the road, outside the house they were aiming for, was Ms Todd. Her summer dress flapped in the breezeless air, bright and colourful and dazzling after the grey, grey, grey of the town.

She wasn't looking their way, so Ember quickly, without thinking, dragged Ness into someone's front garden.

They ducked down behind the low wall.

Grey flowers grew in neat little flowerbeds, poking up from the grey earth, surrounding a grey lawn.

'She said I shouldn't hope,' Ness said, almost to herself.

'There's always hope,' Ember replied. 'I didn't think there was hope when Mr Dedman said your name in assembly the other day, but then look what happened … look where we are. We're together again and I didn't think to even hope for that, it was such a mad idea, but here we are. Sometimes hope turns up when you least expect it.'

'When did you get so wise, Deck?' Ness said, reaching up and almost touching Ember's cheek with her grey fingers.

It was a strange gesture, not one Happiness had ever done before, not when she'd been alive. It was the sort of thing a mother would do, the sort of thing someone sad and saying goodbye might do.

'Dunno,' Ember said, answering the question. 'I just did what I had to do.'

She poked her head out and snuck a glance up the road.

'Has she gone?' whispered Ness.

'I can't see her,' said Ember. 'She's not in the street any more, so yeah, maybe.'

The two girls, the one full of colour and blood and light and nerves, the other washed out and black and white and made of grey, crept up the road, keeping close to the walls of the front gardens.

'It's this one,' Ember said as they reached the house.

The front door was still wedged open, just how she'd left it. All they had to do was go through the house and out the back gate.

It was easy.

So easy.

'We're almost there,' she said, smiling to herself.

'I can't,' said Ness.

She didn't move when Ember pulled her sleeve. She remained glued to the pavement.

'Come on.'

'I can't.'

Ember took a deep breath.

Don't get angry, she thought. *Don't be mad.*

'Look, I know you're nervous,' she said. 'You're probably worried about what we'll say to your mum and dad. But forget that. They'll just be so happy to have you back. They won't even ask any questions.'

'It's not that,' said Ness.

She couldn't take her eyes off the house.

'What are you looking at?' Ember asked.

She was beginning to worry.

She tugged her friend's sleeve again and still she wouldn't move.

'There's something in there.'

Ember looked at the house.

'Ms Todd?'

'Something else,' whispered Ness. 'Her, maybe, but something else too. Something worse.'

Ember thought about what she'd heard as she'd passed through half an hour earlier. What *had* she heard?

'It doesn't matter,' she said. 'We'll just run through. It'll take five seconds. The back door's open.'

And then the front door opened and Ms Todd was there. She was looking over her shoulder, back into the house, as if she were talking to someone.

She bent down to pick up the umbrellas and sticks that blocked the door and she saw the girls.

A strange look crossed her face. Amusement, perhaps? Weariness, maybe?

'You again,' she said, looking Ember straight in the eyes.

'Yes, me again,' said Ember, puffing up tall.

'I did you a favour last time,' Ms Todd said. 'I sent you home, despite the paperwork, despite the promises made. Because it was the *right thing to do*. A *dog*, for *you*? *No!*' She shook her head, almost laughing. An angry, disbelieving, narrow little laugh. 'It would serve you right if I left you this time. *This time* you've got no one else to blame, have you? This time it was *your* doing, *your* idea.

But still, young lady, I'm not ready for you. You're not ready for this. Not ready for here. Not ready for "Goodbye". I am Pity. I am Forgiveness. I am Kind.'

Ms Todd stepped forward, tall and awful, her movements smooth and relentless, like a train clearing the platform.

Ember ran, a sudden wordless cry in her chest urging her on, urging her to get away. Away!

In her panic she knocked Ness over and tumbled across the tarmac herself, before she scrambled to her feet and fled up the road.

She didn't get far before the strong grip of Ms Todd's hand fell on her shoulder.

'December, my dear girl,' the woman said, her breath cold in Ember's ear as she struggled to get free, 'there's nothing you can do to beat me. Listen. It's *not my fault.*'

They plunged together through the water that wasn't there as the worlds changed.

There was the hoot of a car's horn and the sound of brakes.

Ember was thrown to the pavement, rolling in the sure protection of Ms Todd's embrace, out of the path of a staggeringly green car.

It hooted its horn again and screeched off.

'Are you all right?' someone was asking.

'Yes, we're fine, thanks,' Ms Todd was saying. 'These crazy

drivers come out of nowhere without looking. You've got to be so careful these days.'

Ms Todd delivered Ember back to school.

'Out for a dentist's visit,' she explained to Mrs Holland on reception.

'Oh yes, of course,' the woman said. 'How silly of us. We were worried sick. We tried calling your dad but haven't been able to get hold of him. Thought you'd run off.' She giggled a silly, high-pitched little giggle. 'You'd best get back to class, December, it's almost lunchtime.'

Mrs Holland didn't even ask who Ms Todd was. She didn't even seem quite to look at her. But her words had worked. Ember wasn't even in trouble.

She might not be in trouble, she thought, but she wasn't done yet.

She still had the magic map thing in one pocket, and Uncle Graham's back door key in the other.

Despite Ms Todd, she'd keep trying until she'd brought Happiness back.

Ember wasn't about to give up on her friend.

Not yet.

Not now.

Not ever.

The rest of the day went by slowly.

There was a bubble of excitement in her chest that she fought to contain.

Everyone else was still quiet and Happiness's death still echoed in the school, dulling everything. And it echoed most especially in the classroom they'd shared. There was an empty space on their table and the poem Ness had written about Easter was still on the display board. (They'd all written poems, but only the best ones had been pinned up.)

December wanted to stand up and shout, 'She'll be back soon! Tomorrow, she'll be back here! I promise!' but she didn't.

🐾

When she got home that afternoon, Penny let her in.

'You OK? Nice day at school?'

'Where's Harry?'

'He's had to go see a client,' she said. 'A last minute thing, but he should be home before you're in bed. You've got me cooking you tea. I hope you don't mind?'

She didn't mind. The only thing that Penny could cook was hot dogs, the sort you boil for four minutes. Anything that required more complicated cooking than that became inedible. Ember liked hot dogs.

While Penny got the water on to boil, Ember chopped an onion and put some oil in the little frying pan.

'You be careful with that,' Penny said.

There was a broken pair of old dark glasses in the kitchen drawer (they only had one arm) and Ember put them on to stop the oil from spitting in her eye.

'Safety first,' she said, dropping the shredded onion into the pan.

The sizzling was lovely, the smell mouthwatering and the hot dogs slightly overboiled, though you hardly cared once you hid them under ketchup (not mustard) and onions and swaddled them in soft white rolls.

It was only once they'd finished their tea and had wiped their hands and mouths and Ember had swapped her now rather food-stained school shirt for a clean T-shirt that she noticed the card half hidden under a pile of half-opened post on the sideboard.

It looked like an invitation, the sort of card you got from a friend telling you about a birthday party, saying what time and where and whether it was fancy dress or not. Except it was colourless. It was white and silver and simple and had the date of Happiness's funeral in it. The following Monday. It was Thursday evening now. She needed to get Happiness back before then, she thought. Even though she knew a funeral wouldn't make Ness any *more* dead, for some reason it felt like a deadline to her.

🐀

December was sat on her bed in her dressing gown, drying her hair with a towel. She'd just had her bath and other than the bathroom, which still rolled steamy air out on to the landing, the house was cold. Harry said it was immoral to have the heating on at this time of year.

There was a banging on the front door.

She jumped when she heard it.

She glanced at the window. It was already getting dark outside. Why didn't they ring the bell?

Bang.

Bang.

Bang.

She heard her dad stacking plates in the kitchen. He'd come

home while she was in the bath and had shouted a hello through the door, but she'd not seen him yet.

His footsteps crossed the hall as she scooted herself across the bed to look out at the street.

She could hear raised voices in the hall, someone shouting words she couldn't quite make out and Harry answering in a quieter, kinder voice. What was that all about?

She pressed her face to the glass and tried to see down.

She couldn't see who it was at the door, but there was something in the garden, something low and squat and animal-like moving around in the shadows by the front wall. It staggered as if it were uncertain on its feet. The shrubs and flowers shuddered as it banged into them, like a lamb climbing up on to all four legs for the first time.

And then she looked up and she saw the house across the road. The lights were on upstairs and the woman who lived there, a young woman with a baby and a boyfriend and two cats, looked out at her from the window of the big bedroom. Ember thought she smiled as she drew the curtains. And Ember remembered old Mrs Miłosz, who'd lived there before. Then she heard the front door slam and she looked back down to the garden and saw Uncle Graham walk away, and poor, pitiable, not-alive Betty fell out of the shadows after him, limping and hobbling and trailing grimness behind her.

Graham leant on the wall as he went out on to the pavement. He glanced up at the front of the house, and his red eyes roved across it.

She ducked backwards, falling flat on her bed with a bounce.

Had he seen her?

She knew she didn't want him to know she'd seen him, didn't want him to know she'd been watching.

And then there was a soft knock at her door.

'Ember, you decent?' Harry asked.

She sat up and pulled her dressing gown around her.

'Yeah,' she said.

Harry opened the door, came in, sat on the floor by the bed.

'The weirdest thing just happened,' he said. 'Did you hear?'

'Uncle Graham?' she asked. 'I saw him out the window.'

'Yes. Did you hear what he said?'

'No.'

'The poor man,' Harry said. 'He was raving. He must have been drinking. I don't think I've ever seen him drunk before. It's so sad, what some people become. What sadness does to them.'

'What did he say? He sounded angry …'

'Oh, you mustn't pay any attention to him, love. He's upset. He loved his Betty like she was his best friend. I don't think that he has many friends. Your mum said he was a lonely one, even back when they were kids. They grew up in that house of his, you know.

While your mum went off travelling and partying and loving the world, he stayed behind looking after their parents and tinkering with his motorbikes.'

It was nice to hear about her mum. Ember imagined her young and dancing on some tropical beach, flowers in her hair and the white crests of waves crashing on to the sand behind her. She was lovely, and suddenly Ember missed her in a way she'd not done for a long time. She missed her like she missed Happiness.

'He went on about how Betty won't stop following him about. Won't leave him alone. How she's alive and dead and alive again. Weird stuff. I think poor Betty being knocked down's knocked him for six. I hope he can find some help.' He put a big, warm hand on December's knee and looked up into her face. 'Look, you keep away from him for a bit, OK? If you bump into him, just give him a smile and then come home, OK?' He shook his head. 'I'm sure in the morning he'll have sobered up, and if he remembers what he said, he'll be dead embarrassed probably, but all the same … Be safe, Ember. OK?'

She patted Harry's big, warm hand.

'Of course,' she said. 'Of course I'll be safe.'

🐈

Before she went to bed she unfolded the map on the desk where she did her homework.

It was cold, like it wasn't made of paper, but of metal or stone or something.

Looking at the spiral path's strange slow twist made her giddy.

On top of it she laid the key to Uncle Graham's back door.

The questions that she didn't know the answers to were:

Will the map lead me through the alleys, even if I don't start from Uncle Graham's house?

Does the map only work in that alley, or might it work somewhere else too?

Will Happiness be waiting where I last saw her, at Uncle Graham's house, or will she be back on her own front step?

(And the question she almost didn't dare to think: *How can I stop what happened to Betty from happening to Ness?*)

That last question she pushed to the back of her mind. Too terrifying. She'd not thought it, or had managed to ignore it when she'd tried to rescue Ness that morning, but the shadow of it had grown in her mind, the seriousness of it.

Despite that, somehow, eventually, thoughtlessly, sleep took her hand and sank with her into darkness and silence and peace.

·FOURTEEN·

In the middle of the night December woke up.

There'd been a noise on the stairs.

It was pitch black and she couldn't move.

She was lying on her side under the duvet and now there was something in the room and she couldn't move a muscle.

She strained and heaved but her limbs were like lead, like stone. She stared at the wall, at where she knew the wall was in the darkness. Her back was to the door, to the room, and something was moving towards her.

She could hear footsteps – quiet, tiptoeing – tiny footsteps, and she wanted to scream, wanted to shout for her dad, wanted to make a noise to let whoever it was know that she knew they were there, wanted to hurl the duvet off and make a noise and scare them away.

But she was frozen.

Her heart thumped.

She could feel tears tickling over the bridge of her nose.

Lead.

Stone.

A statue.

Paralysed.

Petrified.

And then something landed on the bed.

Thud!

Something had jumped up and landed on the bed, in the dark.

Something had sat down beside her.

And then something cold touched her forehead, touched her ear, touched her cheek.

Cold and wet.

And a voice said, 'I see you.'

Ember sat up in bed, in the dark, her knees tucked up under her chin and the duvet wrapped round her.

In the darkness she could just make out the shape of the cat in front of her.

As it moved its head its eyes glinted, damp and shining.

It spoke and she listened.

Its voice was kind, firm, honest, sharp, but reserved. A short distance away from being warm.

'I know what you're thinking,' it said.

'I can hear you across the town,' it said.

'No good will come of it,' it said.

'You can't do it,' it said.

'Things are the way they are,' it said.

It licked its paw and worried at its ear.

Although she couldn't see it now, she remembered the ragged look of the ear, the ragged look of the cat. As if it had been dragged backwards through a hedge, a ditch and a scrub of cacti and hadn't bothered to comb its hair afterwards.

She didn't think a little lick and brush of the ear would be enough.

'Things are the way they are *for a reason?*' she said, half asking a question.

The cat stopped washing.

'No,' it said, after a moment. 'No reason. They just are, and that's all there is to it. Some things you just have to accept and move on from.'

'But she didn't deserve to die,' Ember said.

'No,' said the cat. 'Few do. But she died, all the same.'

'But I've seen her. I can bring her back. Bring her back here.'

'You've not seen her,' said the cat. 'All you've seen are echoes. Just an echo. You think too much. You think *so* much. You people. I. I. I. Me. Me. Me. All the time. It rings in the world like a bell. It takes a while to fade away, that's all. *Cogitatis ergo estis.*'

'What does that mean?' she asked.

'It means it takes a while to forget that *you* were *you.*'

'That place … ?'

'It's where forgetting happens, that's all. Echoes. Echoes. Echoes. Your people echo longest, that's all. Nothing more.'

Ember thought of the snail she'd watched turn to dust and blow away.

'Snails?' she asked.

'Think very little of themselves,' said the cat immediately.

Hardly even know that they *are*. Only that they *do*. No self-reflection in a snail's mind.'

'Betty? The dog?'

'Dogs think of themselves more, yes. It's all: *Does he love me? Why can't I see him now? Have I upset him? When will he get here?* Awful things, all their thoughts tangled up in their humans.'

The cat looked away, licked its shoulder. Stopped licking.

Ember nodded. She thought she understood. Then she thought of a different question.

'And Ms Todd ... is she ... ?'

The cat said nothing, but jumped down from the bed.

It padded across the floor, its feet soft, its tail crooked in a sudden shaft of moonlight between the curtains.

'Do not do what you are going to do,' it said, as it reached the door. 'She isn't your friend, and I won't be there to help next time. I'm busy. I can hear mice, voles, rats ... Warm. Crunchy. Thinking of themselves just enough.'

December wondered who the 'she' was. Did the cat mean Ms Todd or Ness? Or both?

🐾

She sat there in silence, in the dark, long after the cat had gone, thinking.

Her dad got up.

She heard him banging into things and swearing softly as he made his way to the bathroom.

The toilet flushed.

On the way past her room he stuck his head round the door.

'Oh, Ember,' he said. 'Did I wake you up?'

'No,' she said. 'I was just thinking.'

'Always thinking,' he said. 'Just like her. So smart, so full of ideas. You don't get that from me.' He paused. 'She could've changed the world, you know. If she'd been given the chance. Changed it all round ...'

He scratched at his pyjamas and came and sat on the floor beside the bed.

'Lie down,' he said. 'Shut your eyes.'

And, leaning on the mattress, with his fingers in her hair, he told her all about his day at work and the changes his client wanted made to the plans and how one sort of plasterboard is much better than another, but how, because it's more expensive, he was having a hard time making ...

But by then she was asleep and dreaming of nothing.

Friday was a school day like the rest and December stayed in class, stayed at school all the way through.

She hadn't given up on Happiness though; it was just that now she had a better plan. Or a better start of a plan. Possibly. So long as she didn't look at it too closely.

That evening Harry and Penny were going out. They had tickets to the theatre to see a long play about people sat in a room arguing about who was in love with who. The play had been a hit a few years earlier, but this was the first time it had been put on nearby, so they'd jumped at the opportunity. The tickets had been pinned to the corkboard in the kitchen and the date had been circled on the calendar for ages.

Despite all that, Harry had sat down with her at breakfast and said, 'Ember, if you don't want us to go, we won't. If you want me to stay with you tonight, I will.'

He was a good man, she knew that, and he really wouldn't have minded if she'd said, 'Stay here.' He was really very sweet.

But, as it happened, she didn't want him to stay. Her plan needed him to go.

His mum and dad, Tilda and Porkpie, her gran and grandad, were going to be babysitting (even though she wasn't a baby), and that was going to give her all the opportunity she needed.

*

Tilda and Porkpie weren't like most grans and grandads she knew of.

They were old people made more like teenagers.

Ember wasn't sure what had gone wrong with them, but they'd failed to grow up properly.

After they'd hustled her upstairs ('I'll read for a bit, then go to bed,' she'd told them), they put popcorn in the microwave and snuggled up on the sofa to watch a movie they'd brought over.

Six months earlier Ember had come downstairs to get a glass of water or something, and had found them ignoring the movie entirely while cuddling and giggling and snogging. It had been absolutely horrible.

They hadn't noticed her and she'd snuck back upstairs, embarrassed, surprised and feeling ever so slightly sick.

It had been bad enough when she'd interrupted Harry and Penny, but at least they weren't *really old* and married and didn't smell of talcum powder, and at least they'd been *embarrassed.* Tilda and Porkpie had been together for *decades,* so quite why they were still so lovey-dovey she couldn't imagine, and she didn't want to ask. She just knew Porkpie would say something excruciating like, 'Phwoar, but I don't half fancy your gran something rotten, love,' because that was how he spoke. Embarrassingly.

But still she sort of liked them and they could be fun to go and stay with at Christmas, and, most importantly, they fitted perfectly with her plan for tonight.

Twenty minutes after they'd started their film, Ember slipped silently down the stairs, dressed and in her coat, and, under cover of
    explosions roaring out of the TV
    and kisses spilling from the settee,
    crept out of the front door,
    popping Harry's spare keys into her pocket.

She felt amazing.

Buzzing.

She walked through the streetlight-lit streets as if she did this every evening.

Head up. Confident.

There were teenagers on bikes outside the newsagent's.

A bus passed by, an illuminated room gliding down the road.

The air was cold and there were a few speckles of rain in it.

She slipped into the alley behind Uncle Graham's house and pulled the map from her pocket.

Was it going to work? Was just holding the map enough to make the corners appear for her to go round? Were there other rules?

She stood in the alley and it looked perfectly normal. A dead end at one end, the way out to the street at the other.

Even shutting her eyes and opening them again, even turning around and then turning back didn't change it.

The map chilled her skin, like holding a box of fish fingers straight from the freezer.

She turned the handle on Uncle Graham's gate. Maybe the map would only work its magic if she started from where she'd started before, from *that* back garden, by walking through *that* gate.

She pushed it open carefully and peered around.

The kitchen light wasn't on, but one of the upstairs lights was. A shadow was moving about in the room up there.

The garden was dark and she didn't think whoever was there (presumably her uncle, but you never knew) would see her, not if she was quick.

She took a couple of steps on to the mud that should've been a lawn and took a deep breath.

Pause.

Then she turned round and took a couple of steps back to the gate and went through it into the alley.

The map shivered in her hands like a kitten beginning to purr in its sleep.

She turned left and – yes! – ahead of her was the junction.

She ran round the corner, and then round the next one and the next, her heart keeping steady in the same way a girl walking a tightrope's does: arms wide, eyes shut.

As she passed the fourth corner she wondered where the cat was. It had normally seen her by now, normally made a comment of one sort or another. But not today.

In a way she felt relieved. It would only have tried to talk her out of this again. But at the same time she half missed it. It seemed to be on her side, more so than anyone else, even if it didn't agree with her plans.

But it wasn't there today.

Round the next corner and she pushed her uncle's gate open for the second time in a couple of minutes and there she was, back in the life-leeched black and white world. Dusty and drear.

It looked to be the same grey early evening it always was there.

She stepped from the darkening alley into thin, insipid daylight.

The back door was shut, but not locked this time. (Was that how she'd left it?)

As she tiptoed through the empty house she remembered, with a shiver, what Ness had said: '*There's something in there.*'

The rustling, shifting sound she had heard before didn't come again. There was a faint crackle in the air, but all else was silence.

She hurried on.

She wedged the front door with the umbrellas and walking sticks, as before.

And she froze.

A bumblebee battered itself against the window of her chest.

She was filled with a sudden fear, a sudden flood of uncertainty.

Get Ness, she told herself. *Get Ness and get out of here.*

But, standing in the hallway, about to go out into the world, she felt like she was being watched.

The stairs reared up beside her. Was there someone up there?

And then – a noise from the front room.

Something shifting, something settling in place.

No footsteps.

No voice.

A humming, though, a hint of someone singing to themselves inside their head, and a faint, distant crackle in the air all around her.

Without turning to look, she jumped out into daylight, into the disappointing grey sunshine.

Ness wasn't in the front garden, wasn't waiting in the street for her, but nor was Ms Todd, so Ember turned left and headed off to their own houses.

Only once, walking those empty streets, did she see anything moving.

As she passed the school, something looped across the playing fields.

It was a squirrel, a dead squirrel, bouncing over towards the trees.

It saw her as she saw it and froze in place.

It looked at her, clutching its tail to its chest like an embarrassed woman with a handbag.

'Hello,' she said.

It didn't reply, but after having judged her to be no rival for ghost-nuts or phantom-acorns, or whatever squirrels ate in that dead world, it sprang off, bouncing across the field until it reached the tree, and wrapped itself around the trunk in spiralling loops, right up into the branches and out of sight.

So, she thought, *squirrels remember themselves longer than snails.* She didn't know what she would do with this information, but she stored it away, like an acorn.

What the scientists or psychologists would've given, she thought years later, looking back, to be able to come here and make a study of which animals hung around longest, which had the greatest dose of self-consciousness. But she wasn't a psychologist or a scientist … not yet.

Soon she was stood outside Happiness's house, yet again.

Happiness was back on her doorstep. Back in place. As if she'd never moved.

Did she look even fainter, even greyer, even more washed out than before? Maybe. Maybe.

It was hard to say. From the very first time December had found her here she'd been grey and washed out. Was she fading, or just waiting for a switch to flick from 'echoing' to 'silence'? The snail had been there, and then vanished – the robin too.

It was this place: it sucked the joy out of you.

Ember hoped that taking Ness back to the real world would fill her up with life and light and energy again. Everything that made Ness Ness.

'Deck?' Ness said quietly, without much surprise. 'I thought it was you.'

'I said I'd be back,' Ember said, and she found that her voice wobbled halfway through and the last word choked in her throat.

She felt her eyes growing misty.

'I said I'd come back,' she tried again.

'Thank you,' said Ness.

She stood up slowly, climbing to her feet like it was a great effort.

'We're going to have to be quick,' Ember said. 'We're going back the way we went before, but this time we won't get –'

'Won't get *what?*'

'– caught raid Ember as she turned to look at Ms Todd.

'Ah,' said the woman.

She wasn't smiling any more.

'You shouldn't be here. I have warned you and saved you and sent you home and warned you again, but you insist on coming back.'

'Of course I keep coming back,' Ember said. 'How can I leave her here?' She pointed at Happiness. 'She's my best friend. This is what friends do.'

Ms Todd gave Ness barely a glance as she spoke.

'*It's* not anything. There are no *friends* here. This isn't that sort of place, December, my dear girl. That business is all over the moment you step through my gates.'

'No,' said Ember. She was bubbling inside, boiling like a kettle. 'No, that's not true. She's my friend … here, there and everywhere. *Anywhere. That* don't change.'

Ms Todd dismissed her with a wave of her hand.

'I can't be your protector any more. I'm busy. We are done. It's over. I'm sorry.'

She snapped her fingers, turned on her heel and strolled away up the street.

Ember shivered.

She'd been ignored, left as if she didn't matter.

It felt odd.

She felt odd.

Then she happened to look up, and across the street she saw the net curtain fall back into place as Mrs Miłosz stepped away from the window.

How long had she been watching? Ember wondered, and then she went to glance at her watch.

And she stopped.

Her heart stopped in her chest.

Her breath stopped in her throat.

Her mind stopped thinking; thoughts drifted to the ground like snow and lay unmoving around her feet.

Her watch, her wrist, her hand, her sleeve, her fingers were all drained of colour.

She was black and white.

She was shades of grey.

She was like Ness.

Like the world.

She

was

dead.

'Oh, Deck, you're …' began Ness. Then she stopped.

Ember looked round and, for the first time in this bleached-out, leeched-out, black and white, not-right world, for the first time in the three visits she'd made here, Happiness was smiling.

It didn't matter what she'd been about to say. How she'd planned to finish the sentence she hadn't finished. Whether she'd been about to say 'dead' or 'black and white' or just 'like me', Ember recognised, and understood, that the sadness in the words was overcome, overwhelmed, by the fellowship, by the welcome, by the we're-together-again-ness of them.

She couldn't really, shouldn't really, blame Happiness for that, should she?

How lonely must she have been here all by herself?

Now they were together again.

Forever.

Or for as long as it took them to forget they'd ever been alive.

Dust on the wind, Ember thought. *Soon enough we'll be dust on the wind.*

But however much she understood Ness's words and her smile, she found it made her angry. Angry and sad.

She wanted to kick things. Wanted to break things. Wanted to shout the rudest words she knew at Ms Todd.

She wanted her dad.

Harry, where are you?

And she knew that if he knew about this place, he'd've been here in a shot, breaking down the walls between worlds, running through alleys, bursting through doors in order to rescue her. Just like she'd come to rescue Ness.

But he didn't know. There was no way he'd ever find her.

And then she wondered how it looked, back in the real world.

Ness had fallen off the swing. Someone had found her and they'd rushed her to hospital and she'd died, leaving a body back there and sending a different part of her here.

But when Ms Todd had done the trick on Ember, her body had been here. There was no body in the real world. She would just be missing, lost and gone, whereabouts unknown forever.

Would Harry think she'd run away, gone missing and never come home?

Oh.

That thought, the thought of Harry not knowing where she was, of him forever wondering without finding an answer, was like turning to ice. She shivered with it. She felt the world plunge down the other side of the rollercoaster, her stomach levitating and empty and complaining.

Was it my fault? he'd think.

Oh.

'I'm glad you're here,' Ness said, breaking the spell of her thoughts. 'I was lonely. I was afraid. But now ... now we're together again.'

She'd sat back down and was holding her hand out to Ember, gesturing at the spot on the step next to her. *Sit down*, she was saying, *sit down and stay.*

'No,' snapped Ember, who hadn't given up. 'No, we've got to go. Get up. Get up. There's still a way out, a way back.'

Ness shook her head.

'I don't think so. I'm too tired. Come and sit down. I'm cold.'

'Gah!'

It was frustration. She didn't like being angry with her friend; who did? But why was Ness being like this?

Yes, it had turned cold. Yes, she too felt tired, like a little nap wouldn't be so bad. But … they needed to get moving.

Ember pulled Ness up by the hand.

'Come on,' she said.

Ness didn't resist, but as soon as Ember stopped pulling, Ness stopped moving.

'I can't,' she murmured.

With her arm linked through Ness's arm, Ember marched her friend up the road.

It was slow-going.

Not just because they were arm in arm, and not just because they were tired, but because they seemed to be heading uphill.

138

There'd never been a hill here before, and if you looked you couldn't see one now, but that was how it felt.

And as they walked Ember noticed other ways in which the world seemed to have changed – changed with the change that had happened to her.

Someone had turned the lighting down: the whites of the black and white seemed dimmer, greyer, grimmer, and the blacks sharper, deeper, darker. It was as if night were falling, but the black sun still hadn't moved in the sky.

Either side of them a faint mist rolled that you could only see out of the corner of your eyes.

And the silence was no longer as silent.

Far off there was a sound like a continual rolling thunder or a moaning, or the shuffling of waves on a shore, or a train passing by in the deep of a summer's night. It was a mournful, dispiriting sound, whatever it was.

And inside Ember's chest her heart didn't beat.

There was no pulse at her wrist or neck.

Sometimes she forgot to breathe, and minutes went by and then she noticed and took a deep breath and it made no difference. Breathing was something the dead didn't need to do.

She felt like crying, but didn't. Dead tear ducts are dry.

The anger she had felt at first had long since evaporated

All she felt now was a numbness, a blanketing boredom. And she knew, at last, how Ness had felt all along, all this time.

The girls said nothing as they walked past the school and the bakery and the newsagent's, nothing or nothing much.

Knowledge had arrived in Ember's mind when her life had vanished.

The dead know things.

She knew, for example, that there was no way out, no way back, no resurrection available.

That fact sat inside her like a twin sister, whispering to her.

Going through the gate, back to the colour of the alleys, would do to her what it had done to Betty. She would be not-dead and not-alive. The worst of both worlds.

Balance was the only thing that would work.

A swap. A deal. A trade.

A life for a life.

A death for a death.

One in. One out.

She didn't mention this to Ness. Didn't let on that this was all in vain. Was pointless, fruitless, hopeless. Had always been so.

She guessed Ness already knew.

The other thing Ember knew, though, was that if she stopped moving, if she stopped trying, then she would lose herself, lose all will to do anything.

And it would be so easy to stop.

So easy.

She felt bored and tired and cold.

She felt like she didn't care any more.

She told herself she cared.

Kept telling herself that.

But, really, she just wanted to close her eyes.

Being dead was so easy.

Just close your eyes.

Let go.

Go.

Eventually they turned into Uncle Graham's street.

It had been an effort.

The greyness was everywhere.

'Can't we just sit down?' Ness whispered. 'You and me, Deck. You and me. Just sit down over there. I'm so tired.'

She pointed at a shadowy patch of tarmac beside the sign that said the road's name, much like any other patch of tarmac.

'Of course we can't,' said Ember. 'We're so close. We'll be home soon.'

'I can't go home,' said Ness. 'I just want to sleep.'

Not in a million years would Ember admit that she felt the same urge.

It was like late at night, under the duvet, when the lights were out and the house was quiet and there was a CD playing with a story softly rolling out into the dark. She felt a moment now she'd be dreaming.

But at the same time she was cold, like the duvet was a winding sheet, damp and musty.

'Come on,' she said, pulling Ness up the road.

A cat-shaped smudge appeared in the air from nowhere, and in a second a dead mouse scuttled into its short afterlife, hopping away from the thing that had hitched a ride to the afterworld on the dying rodent's coat-tails.

The cat glowed, bright and multicoloured.

A searchlight had been switched on, a torch that shone in Ember's eyes.

Instinctively she lifted her arm to block the light.

'You?' she said.

'Me,' said the cat.

Ember snuck a look between her fingers.

The colours, the browns and dirty greys and patches of scuffed white and muddy orange, were dazzling, but slowly her eyes grew accustomed.

Although it was hard to look directly at the cat, she could glance at it and keep it at the edge of her vision without too much effort.

'You said you wouldn't come,' said Ember.

'A cat may change its mind,' said the cat.

The words 'A *cat may look at a queen*' came into her head and

she wondered why, where they were from … Was it a nursery rhyme?

'You've done it now,' the cat said. 'I warned you. She's not to be toyed with, that thing.'

'Ms Todd?'

The cat didn't answer the question, but said, 'What are you going to do now?'

'I don't know exactly,' she said. 'But I've still got that magic map thing. I'm gonna try to take us back.'

This was a lie, but she didn't know what else to say. The alternative was to sit down and forget everything.

'It won't work.'

Ember knew that.

'I've got to try.'

'Yes,' the cat said, rocking back and lifting one hind leg up high so it could nibble between the toes.

'Why do you say it won't work?'

She already knew, of course, but asking the question gave her something to push against. Something to feel.

'Rules,' said the cat, between mouthfuls. 'Always rules. In this world, in that world. Life has rules. Death has rules. The universe has rules.'

'Uncle Graham broke the rules,' she said. 'He came and got Betty.'

The cat said nothing, but moved on from its foot to its bum.

Ember knew what it meant, of course, even if she didn't want it to be true.

'Balance,' she said. 'That's a rule, isn't it?'

The cat made a noise that either meant 'Yes' or 'This bit's hard to get clean so I'm giving it an extra hard lick-nibble'.

She'd known it, of course.

They were both dead and they were both stuck.

The cat was right.

'How come you're here?' she asked again.

The cat lowered its leg, sat up straight, licking all round its mouth. It looked at her, its odd-coloured eyes blinking slowly.

'I like you,' it said with something like a shrug in its voice, as if it weren't a big deal, as if it didn't mean much.

It licked a front paw and rubbed it twice across an ear and an eye.

'Five minutes,' it said. 'Come to the house in five minutes. And be ready.'

With that it turned around, stepped behind itself and vanished.

Ember waited for Ness to say, 'What was that all about?' But she didn't say anything.

She'd let go of Ember's arm while the cat had been talking and had wandered away, not far, just over to the side of the road.

'Five minutes,' Ember said, looking at her watch.

The second hand didn't move. It read half past eight, the tim she'd run down the alleys and into this place. She had no how long had passed since then, what time it would be back home now.

She hoped it wasn't too late.

She didn't want Harry to worry.

As they stood outside the house and looked at it, Ember felt something weird happen to her. It was as if her heart had beaten, just once, in her chest, and all the blood that had been sitting still in her veins had suddenly moved round. She shuddered.

She was being watched.

There *was* something in the house.

(She felt a shiver, a falling in her empty stomach. There was something wrong. A well that plunged into the dark below. Or meat left too long on the side.)

The front door was still propped open with the walking sticks and umbrellas. They looked funny lying there, such ordinary things.

'I can't go up there,' Ness whispered, pulling her arm away from Ember's. 'There's something there. I don't like it.'

'There's nothing there,' Ember lied. 'Come on, the cat's waiting '

Be brave. Go on.

She took a step into the front garden, through the little gate, and stopped.

Was that a twitch of the net curtain? The front room's net curtain?

Had something tapped against the window?

Scraped the glass?

She couldn't say.

Had she seen a face in there?

She didn't think so, just the flicker of movement.

It was hard to know, the world being so dim and shadowy. (Had it grown dimmer and more shadowy as they'd walked here? Since they'd talked to the cat? Maybe. It was just so hard to tell.)

'Look, Ness, we've got to go in there.'

'No.'

'So what if there's someone in there? They're just a ghost, like us. Like what we are. I'm sure they won't do us any harm.'

Ember said the words calmly, even though she didn't believe them, or trust them. Even though she didn't know what they'd do when they got in there, when they got to the back gate. But someone had to take charge. Someone had to be brave. Someone had to be the one who pretended they knew what was going on, and today the job was hers

Who could be in Uncle Graham's house?

Why would anyone choose to spend their afterlife there?

Whose house was this?

It had been her mum's childhood home, the house where Uncle Graham had looked after their parents when they got sick, long before December was born. And before then?

She was cold.

Oh.

As she took a step up the path, a dazzling, startling, shining light, like a motorbike headlight, hurtled out of the open front door, leapt high over the bundle of sticks and landed with the pad of soft feet on the ground.

It was the cat, running.

Ember felt the heat as it zoomed between her legs, and she turned, eyes stinging with the brightness of its aliveness, to see where it went, only to find it sat calmly on the ground beside Ness, looking up at her as if nothing was amiss.

'You're back,' she said.

'It took longer than expected,' the cat said. 'But you waited. Good.'

'What happens now?'

'You go through, December. You go home and it balances.'

There were noises inside the house, coming from behind the front door.

It was pulled open. *Pulled wide.*

Sticks clattered as the pile slumped.

Ember covered her eyes against the new light that burst from the doorway.

It was like a visitation, like a glowing alien emerging from its spacecraft, like an angel from an old myth come to share good news.

'You? You!' shouted a voice, disbelief spilling over the edges.

It was Uncle Graham.

How had he got here?

The cat had brought him.

That answer was easy enough to guess.

And then, from between his legs, a grey shape fell, snapping and chomping and dribbling.

Ember jumped aside and the dog lumbered past at speed, oblivious to her, focused on something else.

There was a hiss and a flash of claws and the dog barked and whimpered at the same time as the cat leapt up on to the garden wall and simply ignored the slobbering thing. It looked the other way. Licked at its front paw.

Betty scratched at the wall frantically, bouncing on her hind legs, but she wasn't tall enough.

'Down girl,' snapped Uncle Graham.

The dog stopped jumping, but growled and whined, paced back and forth, turning in pathetic circles, all the while glaring up at the cat and dribbling ghastly black and white dribble.

Then Uncle Graham looked at Ember properly.

'What's happened?' he said. 'You're all … grey.'

He waved his hand at her, as if showing her herself.

'Ms Todd,' said Ember.

'Her?' he said, in a voice that spat.

'Yes,' she replied.

'She's a lying piece of work,' he said. 'Don't trust her.'

He shook his head.

'No,' Ember said.

As they spoke she had been thinking.

The cat had brought Uncle Graham here for a purpose, for a reason.

Now, here, in the world of the dead, there was a *living person*.

That meant that one of the dead could leave, could go back down the alleys, so long as Uncle Graham remained behind.

Balance.

That was what the cat had said.

But, she thought, the cat wanted *her* to go home. It had brought her uncle here in order to let *her* live again.

Like Ms Todd, the cat wasn't thinking about Ness.

But …

She didn't want to go home *alone*. The *whole point* of this had been to find Happiness, to take *her* back, to *bring* her back. What would the point be if she went back without her very best friend?

And the answer spun in her: no point at all.

'Ness,' she said, turning to the faded girl by the wall, and speaking softly but quickly. 'You need to go through the house. I'll distract my uncle. You run! Go out the back and down the alley. It'll take you home … Quickly, go now.'

Ness didn't move.

'I'm scared,' she whispered, almost too quiet for Ember to hear.

The cat had jumped down and led Betty a merry dance across the road, to the gardens on the other side, and Uncle Graham had followed, trying to keep his dog under control. Trying to keep her safe from this strange and dangerous cat, as he saw it.

But now he had turned, come back towards the girls, huddled in their conspiracy. The colour and light spilt from him, hurting their eyes and making Ness cower.

'What's going on?' he shouted.

Ember thought that he must know what she was thinking. How could he *not* see what her plan was? It was so obvious. Obvious, but the only plan she could think of.

But it seemed he didn't.

'Amber,' he said, 'what's going on? What's all this muttering about?'

He was standing on the pavement, and Betty had slumped herself by his feet.

The girls were in the front garden, the front door behind them.

If they could get in the house, Ember could keep her uncle away while Ness ran for the back door. She could give her friend enough time to get away before her uncle, bigger and stronger than her, got into the house.

Her unbeating heart was light now she'd made her decision.

Ness had a dad and a mum and a big brother, she had cousins who came to visit, lots of grandparents, she was much better at being friends with the kids at school, she was going to be a doctor or a vet or an actor one day … she had so much to live for, so many people who were missing her back home … and all Ember had was Harry … not that this was maths, it wasn't just a sum, balancing this side with that, but Ember wanted more than anything for her friend to be alive again, to no longer be just this shadow of the girl, this echo, this bored grey whisper … and even if that meant she, Ember, wouldn't get to see it, it didn't mean it wasn't still the right thing to do …

What did they call it? When you gave something up to help someone else?

There were clouds around her. Grey. Heavy. Dull.

Forget the word, she thought, *just run.*

'Quick,' she said, pushing Ness ahead of her. 'Run!'

Through the door.

Into the hall.

Tripping, slipping on the clatter of sticks and umbrellas.

The two girls, the two ghost girls, fell and rolled across the floor.

A rattle like hail falling.

December spun in place and began pulling the sticks away.

She had to close the door. Get it shut quick.

She could see her uncle moving from the pavement to the front garden.

Heading for her, for the door. For her.

Through the gap, as she scrabbled frantically, she saw a thought cross his shining face.

That face like a flaming beacon, that face filled with life in this grey place, had a thought on it, a memory, a realisation suddenly settling, suddenly understanding itself at last.

He knew, she knew, that if the front door shut he would be locked out.

And he would be shut here, trapped here, to wither forever among the dead.

He began to run as Ember pulled the last umbrella away and threw herself, from her knees, at the door, slamming it shut.

Crash!

He thudded into it. Outside.

They were safe.

He banged at the door, hammered at it, called her name, but she was safe. For the moment.

She turned to Ness, who hadn't helped her, and saw that the moment of safety had been a short one indeed.

Somehow, perhaps in that last split second when she'd thrown herself at the door, Betty had got in. Running ahead of her master, grey and unnoticed, she had slipped through the closing gap, and now she was growling at Ness, who was lying where she had fallen on the hall floor.

Circling round, staring and snarling, the dog dripped grey drops of dribble on to the carpet.

She was between the girls and the kitchen, her wide shoulders blocking the corridor, her grey eyes glinting with violence.

Ness had enough sense left in her to back away, shuffling up the hall, inching away from those jaws that snapped but didn't bite.

Ember climbed to her feet and pushed herself to think.

Had she been alive, adrenalin would have been pumping through her veins, surging her thoughts quicker, her breaths faster, her fear higher, but grey as she was it took effort to even remember the urgency. The need for haste slipped away if she didn't keep reminding herself.

She pinched her arm, like a dreamer.

There was a battering on the front door, and then it stopped.

A moment's silence, and then Betty barked.

She was getting bolder. She wanted her master back, maybe. Was afraid of the girls, maybe. Felt cornered, perhaps

Ember looked around for a way out.

They could run through, run past the dog, for the kitchen, but that seemed too dangerous.

Up the stairs, but that seemed too far, and too dark.

And so, without real thought, simply for a moment's safety, she grabbed Ness by the arm, dragged her up on to her feet and dodged through the half-open door at their side, into the front room.

Click!

The door shut behind her as she leant on it.

Betty banged it from the other side, barked twice, and then there was silence.

Or not quite silence.

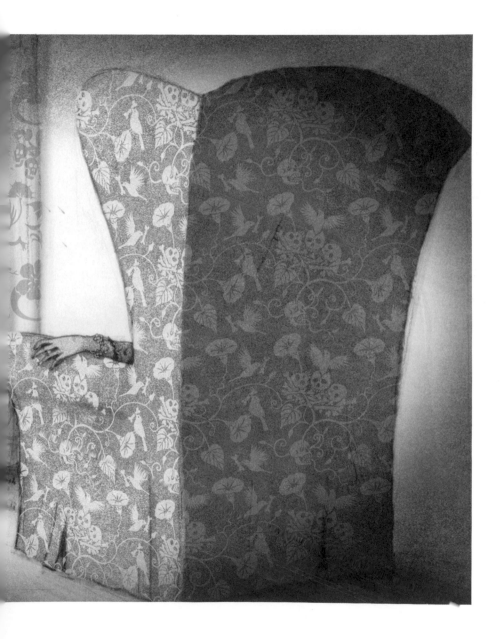

There was the crackle, the hiss in the air that December had noticed in the house before. It came from in here, from this room, and she finally understood what it was.

In the bay window was a television, a big, old-fashioned one that took up a whole table.

Its screen showed static. Black and white dancing.

Facing the television, away from the girls, was a wing-backed armchair, tall, tatty and grey.

All she could see of the occupant was a woman's hand resting on the arm. Pale. Clad in thin, patterned cloth. A bracelet with small stones set in flower-shaped mounts.

For a moment the flowers looked blue, but that had just been a trick of the mind. They were as grey as everything else.

The hand didn't move.

Ness was shaking.

Ember's heart lurched again, a single great pump sloshing blood through her veins.

She felt sick.

Betty barked twice, out in the hallway.

Not knowing why, not understanding her feet, Ember stepped closer … towards the television, towards the chair.

The room was laid out differently from the same room back in Uncle Graham's house. Everything seemed older, from another decade, another century. There was no dog basket.

Ember saw the grey face of the woman in the chair.

Be brave. Go on.

She was watching the static on the TV, gaunt and distant and lost.

She didn't notice Ember.

She was a young woman, but so very dead. A young face, with long dark hair, like someone falling away underwater, drowning and sinking and staring

'What is it?' said Ness.

A whisper.

Nervous.

Shaking.

'It's my mum,' said Ember.

She stood there for a long time, wondering what to do.

Ness lingered in the background.

Just the hiss of static.

21

And then –

A crash at the window. Glass not quite smashing, but cracking, rattling in the frame.

Ember knew she should have jumped. Any red-blooded girl would have jumped at the sudden sound. But her blood was grey, and because she'd been staring so hard at the woman in the chair she hadn't any spare attention to be surprised.

Nevertheless, she looked round.

There at the window Uncle Graham's hands and face were looking in, from beyond the net curtain.

It was like the sun had risen.

Light poured in.

'Gray?'

This, a voice of cobwebs and smoke.

The woman in the chair looked up and a wavering hand

pointed at the window.

'Gray?' she said again.

Uncle Graham vanished, went off looking for some other way in.

Greyness washed the room once more.

In Ember's chest her heart gave another sluggish thud.

'Mum?' she said quietly.

It took a few seconds, years, for the word to cross the gap between them, but once it had the woman in the chair slowly turned her head.

The eyes! Ember thought. *Those are my eyes.*

Another moment passed by with just the hiss of the television for company.

The woman's hair drifted round her head, and her mouth moved soundlessly, searching for the right words.

And then she spoke.

'Em?' she said. 'Is that you?'

'Yes,' said Ember.

'Oh,' said her mother.

A hand lifted up from the arm of the chair, hovered in the space between them.

'You've grown,' she said. 'You've grown so beautiful.'

The words were slow, tiptoed into the air.

Ember didn't know what to say. She didn't move. She didn't breathe.

Her mother looked liked the photos of her, but greyer, lost at the edges.

She was the age she'd been in the photo of the three of them, when Ember was really small.

Yet another surge of blood lurched through her veins, making her feel, making her burn.

She glanced at Ness, but her friend was cowering by the door. She was looking away, looking as if she were about to turn the handle. She didn't want to be there.

Ness had never met Ember's mum. The girls had met years after she'd died.

Maybe Ness wanted to give them some time together, some space. Maybe she was just being polite.

'Mum,' said Ember, 'this is my best friend, Happiness Browne.'

Her mum turned slowly, leant out and peered round the corner of the armchair.

'Both dead,' she sighed, looking from one girl to the other.

'Oh.

Both lost.'

A pause.

'Em, how did it happen? You're so young still. How did you come here so soon? How … ?'

Ember looked down at herself.

She was dead. She'd nearly forgotten, for the moment.

It was almost enough to make you laugh.

'No,' she said, shaking her head. 'I didn't die. No. You see, I'm not *really* dead. It's a mistake, a misunderstanding.'

But she *was* dead.

She explained, as much as she could, what had happened. Ness. Betty. Uncle Graham. Ms Todd.

'And now that cat's helped us,' Ember said. 'The cat's brought everyone here. And I've got to get Ness out the back door before Uncle Graham finds a way in. She's got to go back.'

Her mum stood, tall and desperate, and stepped over to Ness and said, 'Thank you, little one.'

Ness shrank under the words, kind as they seemed to Ember.

And her mum reached down and turned the door handle, which crumbled as she touched it.

The door swung open, just as the front room window exploded in a shower of flying glass, and something huge and solid and real fell to the carpet, shining and shouting with light.

Uncle Graham had got in.

'Ness! Run!' Ember shouted.

Her uncle grabbed her arm.

The burning was intense, there where his fingers touched.

He didn't hold her hard, but just the warmth of his blood, the heat of the life in him, tormented her.

Her thoughts swirled, caught in a flood, confused, confusing thoughts that muddled and bumped together, jostling, making no sense: maybe she could distract her uncle long enough for Ness to get home; or maybe she could distract him long enough for her mum to get home (wouldn't Harry be happy to see her again?); or she could fight free and run home herself, pushing everyone else aside; or she could stay and spend the rest of her dead-life wandering the ghost world, exploring; or she could be with her mum; or her mum could save her, somehow; or Harry could save her; or she could wake up and find that this was all a dream;

or ... oh, Ness!

Her eyes were blurry, not filled with tears, because tears wouldn't come, but with panic and pain.

She sank to her knees.

His burning fingers held her.

'Get away from the door, you,' he was saying. 'Out of the way.'

He was talking to Ness, she thought.

And then there was a whoosh, like a cold wind, that cut through Ember, right to her bones, and he let go of her. His fingers let her slip.

A wind whispered, 'She's mine!'

Ember fell to the floor, crumpled, clutching her arm in her cool, numb hand.

Uncle Graham yelled.

He was flapping wildly, like Hollie Adams did in the play-ground when a bee got too close to her.

Ember looked up and he was wrapped in a ghost, tangled in the seaweed tendrils of her mum's dress, of her arms, her sleeves, her hair. Wreathing and roiling and wrapping. A shipwrecked figurehead refusing to let go.

The light had slowed down.

They were struggling and he was losing, his efforts growing weaker with each moment, with each movement.

Ember couldn't see her mother's face – she had her back to her – but she was afraid of it, all the same.

Gunpowder.

Oh, she understood Ness's fear of the long-dead woman. She was awful, wilful, unforgiving. A pit going down and down, bottomless. Oh! Poor Uncle Graham!

And she shivered with the knowledge of what it was like to touch the living. How Uncle Graham's life, how his blood and breath and heat, burned, scorched … how it hurt. Oh! Her poor mother!

Ice, becoming slush.

And then her mum stepped back, drifted back, let go. Opened her arms and stepped back, and her uncle staggered against the wall, dazed, lost, ashen and gasping for breath.

Pale as a ghost.

He was confusion, forgetfulness, fear.

He pushed himself away from the wall, not looking at anyone, not seeing anyone, not hearing anything but the thud of his heart. And as he pushed he touched Ness, pushed her against the wall under his hand, and she slid away as he fell through the open doorway into the hall …

And then he was gone, vanished off down the passage, to the kitchen, to the garden, to the …

And her mum shrank down, just a woman again, drifting gently with the current; her hair flowing, her eyes looking away.

And Ness continued sliding along the wall, her eyes clear and wide and staring.

'Deck,' she said in a calm, faraway whisper, 'there's something wrong. Something wrong here ... I don't feel ... I don't feel anything ...'

And then she fell to the floor, but like someone sitting down after climbing a long flight of stairs, not like someone collapsing, and she looked up at Ember one final time, her eyes almost brown, and flashing, and then she looked away, distracted, and crumpled, faded, sifted into a girl-shaped heap of dust.

And then the heap itself faded, shrank, blew away, grain by grain, on a wind that Ember didn't feel, on a wind that moved nothing else in the room, that blew from nowhere to nowhere.

'No,' she said, gasping.

'No!'

And then her mother was beside her, in front of her, staring into her eyes.

'Em, dear,' she said in a whisper, 'it's just us now.'

Ember was struggling.

'But ...

Ness ...

she ...'

The words didn't work.

Dust on the wind, said her mother's eyes, which were her eyes.

A pause …

then …

her mum reached down, rippling like kelp, and embraced her.

Held her tight.

Held her there.

Held her forever.

And December's tearless eyes wept for Happiness.

23

Days passed like a dream, held in those arms, lowered, hunched, crouched together on the living-room floor.

At one point Betty waddled into the room.

She looked around, greyness looking at greyness, and sadly waddled over to the pair of them.

Her master had gone.

She'd been left alone again, and being still a dog at heart, alone was the one thing she couldn't bear. Anything but that. Anything but *alone*.

Without asking, without seeming to think anything was strange, Betty waddled forward and slumped with a *crumph* beside them, leaning hard and heavy and cold against Ember's side, and then she laid that big head of hers on the girl's lap.

Her mum gently, idly, stroked the dog's face.

'Such a pretty one,' she whispered. 'Good old Gray.'

And so, then they were three.

And then, after a while, they were two again, as the dog's dust was lifted up on an unfelt wind.

And Ember thought, *She wasn't such a bad dog,* as she wiped ghostly dribble off her trousers. *She was mostly made of love.*

And endless time passed by.

What was left?

Ness was gone and Betty was gone and Uncle Graham had left them all.

He'd run off, out the house, through the garden and back to the real world.

She could feel it.

She'd come here to save Ness, but with Ness gone she could have saved herself. And that had been the cat's plan all along, after all: leave Uncle Graham here and let dead December flee back to the light. But the chance had passed by. The chance had gone.

Her mum was humming, a tune she had never heard before.

'He could have saved you,' Ember whispered eventually.

'What?' said her mum.

'Uncle Graham,' she said. 'He brought me here to get his dog back. To rescue Betty. He made a deal with someone … with that Ms Todd, I think … that let him swap a living person for a dead one.'

Her mum said nothing.

'He could have done it back then, though, couldn't he? He could have saved you. I would've. You know I would've if I could've. I'd've been here in a flash, or Harry would've …'

'Em, darling,' her mum said. 'You were tiny. There was nothing you could do. Nor Harry. And don't blame Gray either. Without him, I'd not ever have seen you again. We wouldn't be together now, would we?'

Rustling leaves. A breeze in autumn. Falling leaves.

'I waited,' her mum said. 'For so long. I held on. Dreaming, perhaps. Days or years or minutes or hours. Time is strange. Look how big you got … How did that happen?' She leant back and brushed a strand of hair away from Ember's eyes, stroked her cheek. 'When did you get so big? Oh.'

Ember felt like she was falling asleep, was warm in bed, although it was cold.

The black and white world around her was dimming, growing fainter. Just a room now. Just them.

She smiled.

'We are together,' her mum said.

'Yes,' whispered Ember.

For years she had wondered if she'd have anything to say to her mum were she ever to meet her. She'd imagined her like a movie star, like someone you know off the telly, who you recognise, who seems so familiar, but who you don't really know at all. Who doesn't know you. She'd expected to be tongue-tied and embarrassed. But it wasn't like that. Not like that at all.

There were things she wanted to tell her mum, about her and Harry, and about school and about holidays, and about Ness, and about moving house, and about Tilda and Porkpie, and about what was happening in her favourite shows on TV, and about what had happened in the soaps her mum had liked in all the years since she'd stopped watching them.

There was so much to say, and she didn't need to say any of it.

Not a word.

She just wanted to sit quiet and safe in that embrace.

They could be quiet together, and that was a gift.

'We've all the time in the world,' her mum said, reading her mind.

It made sense.

Ember felt so sleepy.

Her eyes were closing.

Neither hot nor cold now.

Just dim. Fuzzy.

She'd had her life, hadn't she? She'd been happy. She'd been loved. She'd lived enough, hadn't she? It hadn't been bad.

'Stay with me,' her mum whispered. 'You belong with me. You were always mine.'

Her voice was barely a breath.

'Stay here.'

She began humming that tune again.

Ember slept, or sort of slept, deep in her mother's arms for the first time in what might have been centuries.

And that long night went on.

Eventually, suddenly, the sun rose in December's dream, a startling dawn, too early, filled with birdsong and summer haze. It washed away sleep, comfort, forgetting.

'Get away from her,' said a voice from out of the light.

Ember knew that voice.

She stumbled closer to wakefulness.

Despite the light, despite the summeriness, she felt cold, weighed down.

'Leave her be,' said the voice. 'She is not yours.'

She knew the voice.

She was treading water, struggling to get her head into the air.

There was a hiss and flash of claws and fire and December was thrown up on to the riverbank, and she found she was in the front room, lying on the rug that covered the floorboards, staring at its grey pattern.

The cat was stood between her and her mother, its light spilling out, filling their faces.

She covered her eyes, blinked hard and saw her mother high above her.

'No. Em,' she said, 'we are together again. At last, it's us.'

'Run, girl,' the cat said calmly, firmly, simply. 'Go home. People are waiting for you. Your supper's waiting and it's still hot. Run, now.'

Ember backed away. She saw her mother for what she was, for what she had become: a ghost, long-lost herself, deep underwater.

The cat hissed.

'Too long,' it said, looking at the dead woman.

'Far too long.'

Ember climbed to her feet. Sense climbed into her head.

She wasn't meant to be dead.

This was her last chance to run.
She took a step towards the door,
but there was a knot she couldn't untie.

'I can't,' she said, surprising herself. 'You don't understand, cat. That's my mum.'

'And she's dead, girl,' the cat said, not turning away from the woman. 'And you don't have to be. Look to the living. Look to the living now. It's not your time to be here.'

She was torn in pieces.

'Run.'

She didn't.

'I heard what you were thinking, girl. The word you wanted was "sacrifice", and you would've done it. I can see you. I can see into you. I know you better than you know. You would've done it for her, now I will do it for you.'

'What?'

'I will stay,' the cat said. 'I am alive. You are dead. That is the deal. I will stay; you will go.'

Ember's heart gave a sudden single, surging beat.

'Do not even think to argue.'

Blood heaved in her.

Hope heaved.

'Do not linger.'

She didn't want to stay here.

She didn't want to be dead any more.

'Em,' her mother said, leaning down beside her. 'Stay.'

She laid a hand on Ember's shoulder.

For such a grey and washed-out dead woman, the grip was astonishingly strong, astonishingly tight, astonishingly cold.

Dust and electricity and ice.

Love, turned to an anchor, turned to seaweed, turned to bindweed.

Ember couldn't move.

She tugged, but it was no good.

'Oh,' she said, feeling suddenly, finally, endlessly, defeated.

She looked at the cat.

'It has to be you,' the cat said. 'I cannot do this.'

Ember tried to wriggle free, tried to shake her mother off, but the arms came around her, embraced her, surrounded her.

'Em,' said a whisper in her ear. 'Don't leave me. Don't leave me again.'

Each word was a knife.

'No,' said Ember.

Instinctively she gulped worthless air into empty lungs, like someone about to be dragged under.

'I've been waiting,' her mother whispered. 'You made me wait so long. So long.'

'No,' Ember whispered.

'You can't … you can't leave me. Don't leave me. Not again.'

The arms wrapped round her like smoke, fogging her and choking her. Drowning her. Pulling her. Down, down, down.

She struggled and pushed back helplessly.

Her heart gave another thump; another jolt of blood surged in her veins, burning her insides with life.

And then …

'No!' she shouted. 'No!' She twisted and turned in the icy embrace. 'It wasn't me,' she gasped. 'It wasn't *me* who left *you*. It wasn't *me*. I didn't go away. Mum! It wasn't *me* who left.'

And with that final shout, that expulsion of truth, of heart, of honesty, tears came to her dry eyes and a breeze came up from nowhere and a tickling crossed her arms and face and she collapsed forwards, no longer held up, no longer pinned down. A shadow lifted, a memory flew away, a forgetfulness fell.

And then …

dust

… it was just her and the cat in the front room.

She sat there for a long time as the cat paced and sat and paced and washed.

In time she stood up. Exhausted. Emptied out.

The cat watched as she went to the kitchen.

'Harry's probably waiting,' she said to the room.

The cat nodded. Walked behind her.

In the garden it trotted in front of her, dug in a flowerbed, turned and looked at her.

'I don't expect to see you for a long time,' it said.

'What will you do?' she said.

'This and that,' said the cat. 'Sleep, maybe.'

'But this place,' she said.

The cat looked around.

'All places are alike to me,' it said. 'Here or there, it doesn't much matter. The quiet will be nice.'

She had reached the gate and turned the handle.

The alley was filled with colour.

'Ms Todd?' she said.

The cat said nothing, but it filled in the hole it had made and jumped up on to the fence.

The last Ember saw of it was a flash of colour vanishing into next door's garden like a sunset.

Oh, she thought. I *didn't say thank you.*

She let the gate click shut behind her.

She hurried to the first corner and walked round it, past the bins to the next corner.

She was without Happiness, but somehow that was all right.

It was all wrong, of course, but also it was all right.

As she turned the third corner, her heart started beating again, and didn't stop.

Ember ran through the night.

It was almost eleven o'clock (her watch had caught up with the real world as soon as she'd returned).

She got home just after Harry and Penny.

She hid behind a parked car and watched them unlock the door and let themselves in.

As soon as the door was shut she scampered across, lifted the letterbox flap and peered through.

Harry had gone into the front room and Penny was heading off down the hall through the kitchen to the bathroom at the back.

As soon as she was out of sight, Ember slipped the spare key into the door and, with tiptoeing movements, opened it slowly.

She slipped in and left the door slightly ajar. (To shut it you always had to bang it because the lock was stiff.)

She could hear Harry and her grandparents talking, about the play and about the evening and she heard the words, 'No trouble at all. Not heard a peep all night. Good as gold.'

And at that Ember ran up the stairs two at a time, avoiding the squeaky third step, and was under the covers (with her shoes on) by the time her dad opened her door.

She pretended to sleep.

It was only once he'd kissed her on the head and gone out again that she began to fiddle with her shoelaces.

They had knots and in the end she just slipped them off, still tied, and let them fall to the floor for Harry to deal with in the morning.

Then she lay in the dark and cried, real tears. Wet tears. Salt tears.

Happiness was gone, and she hadn't even said goodbye to her. She was *really* gone and nothing was going to bring her back. Not this time, no matter how clever Ember was, no matter how much she wished it.

There was a hole in her middle, and she fell down it.

She thought of her mum too, as she fell.

She thought of the picture of her on the mantelpiece that she'd always loved, not what she had become. It was surprisingly easy to let go of the memory of what had happened in that afterworld. The knowledge that her mum had waited was enough to know. The rest she could forget. Let go of.

Yes. Letting go. Let it go.

And so she cried.

Big sobs, like the dead deserve.

But, in time, she was all cried out, and she turned her pillow over to the dry side and tried to sleep.

December didn't go to school on Monday, because it was the day of the funeral. The weather was suitably grey and blustery and she wore her smartest, darkest clothes.

There were a few other kids from school there, but she didn't speak to them. She just sat with Harry and Penny and was quiet. It was what she wanted to do.

At the front Mr and Mrs Browne sat quietly too. Ness's big brother had come back from university to be with them. He sat there, in a suit that didn't quite fit, with his head in his hands.

The coffin was brought in and they all stood up and then they all sat down again.

Someone said some words she didn't really hear, and then a cousin of Ness's that Ember had never seen before stood up and sang a song that she'd written for the guitar. And then they all stood up and sang a song, and then they all sat down again. Ness's grandad, who Ember had never met either, stood and said a lot of words about her, about how good she was and how kind and all that sort of thing.

She remembered some of the things Ness had told her, some of the stories she'd told her about him, and she smiled, almost laughed, in fact.

Then they played some music, and the coffin trundled off through some curtains into a hole in the wall and she knew that that was where it would be burned.

Everyone cried, and then afterwards they went to a nearby pub, where the Brownes had laid on some food.

Even though Ember wasn't hungry she ate three sausage rolls, four little triangular sandwiches, a stale salted peanut and several handfuls of crisps out of politeness.

Before they left she went up to Ness's mum, Mrs Browne, and said, 'I'm sorry.'

She didn't know what else to say.

I *tried?*

Mrs Browne didn't need to know that.

She just said, 'Thank you, Amber, dear,' and dabbed her eyes with a soggy handkerchief.

No one corrected her. It wasn't the time.

'Come on,' said Harry quietly, his hand on her shoulder.

They headed for the exit, but halfway there Ember turned and ran back to Ness's mum.

'Mrs Browne?' she asked.

'Yes?'

'Can I ask … ? I've a question …'

'Yes?'

'When they give you the dust, can I –'

'Dust?'

'You know, from the coffin and …'

'The ashes?'

Mrs Browne choked as she said the words.

'Can I … Can you give me a bit? Just a little. She was my *best* friend, and I want to, you know, scatter a bit of her in the garden.'

It was what people did, wasn't it? Harry had scattered her mum's ashes in the woods where they sometimes walked, where the bluebells came out in the spring.

Mrs Browne was silent, as if she didn't know what to say.

'Of course you can,' said Mr Browne, putting a hand on his wife's shoulder. His eyes were huge and shining, still and deep and reflective as hammer ponds. 'Can't she, Hazel? Ember was all that Ness would talk about. She loved you, you know.'

'Of course,' repeated Mrs Browne.

'It'll be a few days,' Mr Browne said. 'I'll bring them round.'

'Thank you,' said Ember, not feeling in the least bad about the lie she'd told them.

She had no intention of scattering Ness's dust. She'd seen her ashes scattered already. She wanted to keep some of it together, keep it safe. That was all. She had no plan to do anything with it. She just wanted to have her friend close.

With a tear rolling down her cheek and a red nose, she walked back to Harry and Penny and took them each by the hand and walked with them out into the car park, out into the cool spring afternoon, out into the rest of their days together. Happy days.

Not to be forgotten.

Not to be rushed through.

Not to be wasted.

Praise for *The Imaginary*

'By turns scary and funny, touching without being sentimental, and beautifully illustrated by Emily Gravett, *The Imaginary* is a delight from start to finish'

Financial Times

'A moving read about loyalty and belief in the extraordinary'

Guardian

'The kind of children's book that's the reason why adults should never stop reading children's books. Touching, exciting and wonderful to look at (Emily Gravett's illustrations are incredible), I absolutely adored this. And I cried a little bit'

Robin Stevens

'A glorious delight … Loved it!'

Jeremy Strong

'Packed full of heart'

Phil Earle, *Guardian*

'This is young fiction of the very best quality, showcasing inspiration, inventiveness and an intoxicating passion for storytelling. *The Imaginary* has the potential to be a family favourite and a future classic'

BookTrust

'A richly visualised story which explores imaginary friends and the very special role they play in children's lives. Emily Gravett's illustrations capture the hazy world of the imaginaries brilliantly'

Julia Eccleshare, Lovereading4kids

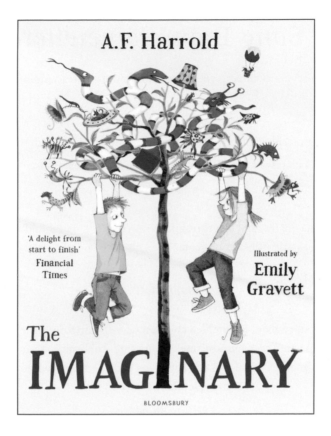

A.F. Harrold

'A delight from
start to finish'
Financial
Times

Illustrated by
Emily
Gravett

The
IMAGINARY

BLOOMSBURY

RUDGER IS AMANDA'S BEST FRIEND.

HE DOESN'T EXIST.

BUT NOBODY'S PERFECT.

Winner of the UKLA 2016 Book Award in the 7–11 category

Longlisted for the CILIP Carnegie Medal
and the Kate Greenaway Medal 2016

Praise for
The Song From Somewhere Else

'Extraordinary … as moving, strange and profound as David Almond's *Skellig*'

Guardian

'Broodingly atmospheric black-and-white illustrations by Levi Pinfold … the tale turns into a fantasy of another world, blending the strange and the everyday'

Sunday Times

'Wildly imaginative and heartbreakingly moving … Levi Pinfold's superbly evocative, misty illustrations complete a glorious and unforgettable tale of loyalty, loss and friendship'

Daily Mail

'A curious story about two bullied children who end up forming an unlikely friendship based on a haunting melody, an improbable mother, an invasion from another world and a disappearing cat. There are wonderfully evocative pictures by Levi Pinfold'

Evening Standard

'What begins as a story of bullying becomes a whirlpool of mystery as Frank tries to undo the damage she has done. A magic story of friendship and love, with atmospheric black-and-white illustrations by Levi Pinfold'

Irish Examiner

'There is a delicate sensibility, a happy strangeness, to this; sometimes scary, sometimes funny, always essential. The illustrations by Pinfold – black and white, pencil, dramatic and evocative – are a vital component'

Big Issue

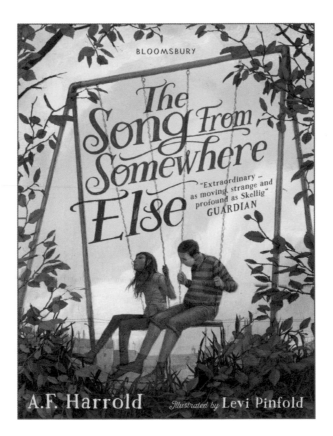

SOMETIMES YOU FIND FRIENDSHIP
WHERE YOU LEAST EXPECT IT.

Longlisted for the CILIP Carnegie Medal
and shortlisted for the Kate Greenaway Medal 2018

Winner of the Amnesty CILIP Honour 2018